GRAVE
INJUSTICE

SEAL Brotherhood: Legacy Series

Book 3

SHARON HAMILTON

SHARON HAMILTON'S BOOK LIST

SEAL BROTHERHOOD BOOKS

SEAL BROTHERHOOD SERIES

Accidental SEAL Book 1

Fallen SEAL Legacy Book 2

SEAL Under Covers Book 3

SEAL The Deal Book 4

Cruisin' For A SEAL Book 5

SEAL My Destiny Book 6

SEAL of My Heart Book 7

Fredo's Dream Book 8

SEAL My Love Book 9

SEAL Encounter Prequel to Book 1

SEAL Endeavor Prequel to Book 2

Ultimate SEAL Collection Vol. 1 Books 1-4 /2 Prequels

Ultimate SEAL Collection Vol. 2 Books 5-7

SEAL BROTHERHOOD LEGACY SERIES

Watery Grave Book 1

Honor The Fallen Book 2

Grave Injustice Book 3

BAD BOYS OF SEAL TEAM 3 SERIES

SEAL's Promise Book 1

SEAL My Home Book 2

SEAL's Code Book 3

Big Bad Boys Bundle Books 1-3

BAND OF BACHELORS SERIES

Lucas Book 1

Alex Book 2

Jake Book 3

Jake 2 Book 4

Big Band of Bachelors Bundle

BONE FROG BROTHERHOOD SERIES

New Year's SEAL Dream Book 1

SEALed At The Altar Book 2

SEALed Forever Book 3

SEAL's Rescue Book 4

SEALed Protection Book 5

Bone Frog Brotherhood Superbundle

BONE FROG BACHELOR SERIES

Bone Frog Bachelor Book 0.5

Unleashed Book 1

Restored Book 2

SUNSET SEALS SERIES

SEALed at Sunset Book 1

Second Chance SEAL Book 2

Treasure Island SEAL Book 3

Escape to Sunset Book 4

The House at Sunset Beach Book 5

Second Chance Reunion Book 6

Love's Treasure Book 7

Finding Home Book 8 (releasing summer 2022)

Sunset SEALs Duet #1

Sunset SEALs Duet #2

LOVE VIXEN

Bone Frog Love

SHADOW SEALS

Shadow of the Heart

SILVER SEALS SERIES

SEAL Love's Legacy

SLEEPER SEALS SERIES

Bachelor SEAL

STAND ALONE BOOKS & SERIES

SEAL's Goal: The Beautiful Game

Nashville SEAL: Jameson

True Blue SEALS Zak

Paradise: In Search of Love

Love Me Tender, Love You Hard

NOVELLAS

SEAL You In My Dreams Magnolias and Moonshine

PARANORMALS

GOLDEN VAMPIRES OF TUSCANY SERIES

Honeymoon Bite Book 1

Mortal Bite Book 2

Christmas Bite Book 3

Midnight Bite Book 4

THE GUARDIANS

Heavenly Lover Book 1

Underworld Lover Book 2

Underworld Queen Book 3

Redemption Book 4

FALL FROM GRACE SERIES

Gideon: Heavenly Fall

NOVELLAS

SEAL Of Time Trident Legacy

All of Sharon's books are available on Audible, narrated by the talented J.D. Hart.

This is a work of fiction. Names, characters, places, brands, media, and
incidents are either the product of the author's imagination or are used
fictitiously. In many cases, liberties and intentional inaccuracies have
been taken with rank, description of duties, locations and aspects of the
SEAL community.

ABOUT THE BOOK

Personal tragedy lands Navy SEAL Armando Guzman into the pits of Hell. Were it not for his three-year-old son, this strong warrior would have ended his suffering with a bullet—either as a KIA or by his own hand.

She is his secret enemy; her heart is filled with revenge and hate.

Will their intense and feisty hookup-turned-relationship assure their mutual destruction, or are each of them the key to the other's healing?

Book 3 of the SEAL Brotherhood Legacy Series. To read the original story of Armando Guzman and his family, read SEAL Under Covers, which takes place ten years prior to the new story.

AUTHOR'S NOTE

I always dedicate my SEAL Brotherhood books to the brave men and women who defend our shores and keep us safe. Without their sacrifice, and that of their families—because a warrior's fight always includes his or her family—I wouldn't have the freedom and opportunity to make a living writing these stories. They sometimes pay the ultimate price so we can debate, argue, go have coffee with friends, raise our children and see them have children of their own.

One of my favorite tributes to warriors resides on many memorials, including one I saw honoring the fallen of WWII on an island in the Pacific:

> "When you go home
> Tell them of us, and say
> For your tomorrow,
> We gave our today."

These are my stories created out of my own imagination. Anything that is inaccurately portrayed is either my mistake, or done intentionally to disguise something I might have overheard over a beer or in the corner of one of the hangouts along the Coronado Strand.

I support two main charities. Navy SEAL/UDT Museum operates in Ft. Pierce, Florida. Please learn about this wonderful museum, all run by active and former SEALs and their friends and families, and who rely on public support, not that of the U.S. Government. www.navysealmuseum.org

IF YOU GOT ANY CLOSER, YOU WOULD HAVE TO ENLIST

I also support Wounded Warriors, who tirelessly bring together the warrior as well as the family members who are just learning to deal with their soldier's condition and have nowhere to turn. It is a long path to becoming well, but I've seen first-hand what this organization does for its warriors and the families who love them. Please give what your heart tells you is right. If you cannot give, volunteer at one of the many service centers all over the United States. Get involved. Do something meaningful for someone who gave so much of themselves, to families who have paid the price for your freedom. You'll find a family there unlike any other on the planet.

www.woundedwarriorproject.org

CHAPTER 1

NAVY SEAL ARMANDO Guzman was at the hospital with his wife, Gina, when he got the call from Kyle.

"We lost Erik today. I wanted you to know."

"Christ, what happened?"

Ignoring the question, Kyle continued, "Christy will arrange for visits from the ladies with meals and offers for babysitting."

Gina's eyes fluttered as her head rolled from side to side. He could see she was either in pain from the cramping or upset at circumstances which brought them here. He quietly tiptoed into the bright hallway.

"Son of a bitch. How?" he whispered his demand.

Sounds of the floor call system blared in the background.

"Where are you?" Kyle asked.

"At the hospital. She lost the baby. Again." He heard the waver in his own voice, and it pissed him off.

"We thought the drugs would help this time, but she started bleeding then cramping. And, well, maybe it's a blessing in the long…"

"God, Armando. I'm so sorry. I shouldn't have called you."

"No. How the hell would you have known? I'm glad you did. We were hoping, but we lost this battle. Not sure if we'll try again. It's Gina's call."

"Always is. She's strong, Armando. And you guys have Artemis, after all. He'll be a blessing to you."

"Tell me how it happened."

"It was a freak thing. They targeted him, saw his long gun, and knew he was our sniper. We thought he was covered well, but someone from the compound we were breaching spotted him before he could adjust his position. Took him right out. He did nothing wrong except not turn into an invisible man. We had a hell of a time getting inside. We got four wounded, but we got 'er done."

"You got the warlord?"

"One of his own men capped him. I think it was an accident. They were scared shitless, running around, disorganized. But someone knew the score. Figured it out."

"Did someone get the shooter?"

"He got away, along with two of the ten hostages. One was executed. We got the other seven back to

Germany safe but really shook-up. It was a mess. They slaughtered most of the village. You could smell the burn pits from miles away."

"I should have been there."

"Nope. Don't go doing that. Your place was at Gina's side. This was Erik's turn. He drew the card. You know how it goes, Armando. We don't make all the rules; the enemy gets a vote. We just hope to get lucky enough to figure it out in time. Erik's time ran out. If anyone is to blame, it's me."

But Armando knew he would have done anything to not be there at the hospital tonight and face the devastation in his wife's eyes after telling her they'd lost their latest. A boy, the doctor told him confidentially, as if that made any difference. It actually made it worse.

He clenched his fist and felt the ice water in his veins. He wanted to go kill something in exchange. He hated hospitals just for this very reason. As a man of action, he didn't do wait. He wanted it all and right now.

Except, at this moment in time, he didn't want anything. Was he even alive?

"Armando? Are you still there?" Kyle barked.

"Of course I'm here."

"Is Gina going to be okay? No complications, I hope."

It was a nice try, but Armando felt like punching him through the phone.

"No. No complications, other than a broken heart."

"Geez, man, I'm so sorry."

"Yeah, well, anything I can do for Erik's—what's her name?"

"Sambra. She'll get the visit in the morning. Christy is going over with them. I don't know them very well, but we're still in Germany for a couple more days, and I think the ladies will take lead on this. We can make the house call later. You just stay with Gina. I thought you should know."

"Thanks, Kyle." He was a tiny bit grateful for the distraction. He'd been sitting there in the near-dark, thinking about what he was going to say to her when she woke up. He was glad Artemis was staying with Armando's mom and, at his age, would be oblivious to the tragedy.

Gina was awake when he entered the room.

"Hey, sweetheart," he said as he sat on the bed and gripped her right hand in his, squeezing it on his bent knee. He hoped his voice was soothing.

But she knew. Her vacant expression told him everything, and that hurt even more than the pain of knowing they'd tried and lost another personal battle. Their relationship was on tenterhooks, and the fire in her eyes had gone out several months ago. She'd been afraid the entire first four months of her pregnancy.

"You would have reassured me if everything was okay. So I guess that means—" She pulled her hand away, curled up into a ball, and turned her back to him, sobbing.

He placed a firm hand on her shoulder, but she shrugged it away.

"Gina, sweetheart, it's not your fault, you know. We've been told this before. This happens when—"

"Oh, shut up, Armando. Leave me alone. Don't soft-pedal it. I can't have children. I know I can't."

"You have one. We have Artemis."

She stayed curled up with the cold arch of her back rising and falling with her sobs. She was inconsolable. He knew she'd work it out in time, and he was going to give her all the time it took. He'd be patient; he'd wait on her hand and foot. Perhaps he'd even get a leave from the Teams and they could take a trip, maybe just the two of them, to ease her pain. If that would help. Right now, he wasn't sure his presence would help her, though.

He rubbed her shoulder, hoping she'd turn onto her back so he could look into her eyes and tell her he loved her. He wanted to do that.

But she didn't move. So he bent over and whispered, "Gina, I love you so much. I'm so grateful for you, that you are okay. I'm grateful for all that we've been for each other for these eight years, sweetheart, for Artemis, for everything."

She remained on her side, covers up to her neck, gripping them under her chin.

"I'm going to be right here. You go to sleep. They told me you can go home in the morning, so get some rest. But I'll be right here beside you. See? They've brought a bed in so I can stay."

"I don't want you here. Go home, Armando."

"You don't mean that—"

She reared up and screamed at him, "I said I don't want you here. Go home!" She pointed to the door. Her face was red, her eyes raging and feverish. Her anguished mouth looked like a knife wound in her face. There was no softness. His Gina was not there.

"Why don't you lie down and just rest? Don't worry about me."

"I don't want to see your face. I don't want to hear you breathe or smell you. You remind me that I can't have your babies!" Her lower lip quivered, and she collapsed into the pillow again.

The evening nurse entered the room with a stern expression, her lips downturned.

"Mr. Guzman, I think it's best if you let her have some alone time," she whispered.

Armando could see she was an old hand at this sort of thing. She wasn't a very attractive woman, but she knew how to make things better, and that made her an angel of mercy. He was glad she'd be watching over Gina all night long.

"Go home and get some rest yourself." She leaned into him and whispered, "Everything looks better in the morning with the new sunlight. You'll see." She gave him a wink of the wise.

He was powerless to fight both these women.

ON THE DRIVE home, he called his mother and gave her the news. Felicia sounded strong, but he could tell she was heartbroken.

"It is for the best. It will happen when it happens. Don't worry about it, Armando. She'll be right soon enough," she said to him in her pigeon English, which told him that her husband, Gus, a former San Diego Police Sergeant, was sitting close by listening.

"You're right, of course, Mom. I'm going home to get some rest, and I'll pick her up in the morning."

"I will bring her some fresh flowers from the garden tomorrow when I bring over Artemis. Don't worry about it, my son. You will see. Gina will heal. Little Artemis has been a diablo and nearly worn Gus to the ground, so I'm glad you will be there. You'll need to talk to him, Armando. He needs discipline. He's very spoiled."

He agreed with her. He heard whispering in the

background.

"Do you need us to keep him one more day? We'd be glad to." She giggled after she said this, indicating to Armando that it was a complete lie.

"Mama, I thank you, but no. I think Gina will soak up his energy. And yes, I'll talk to him."

He played some somber jazz as he completed his drive. Uncharacteristically, it started to rain. He could count on one hand the number of times it rained in April in San Diego, but it rained tonight.

So be it.

CHAPTER 2

GINA WOKE UP to the intense light of the morning sun. It was always brighter on this side of the hospital. She was unhappy realizing that today she would've rather been on the shady side. But they liked to put her over here. As if the sunlight could improve her mood.

"I ought to get used to this by now," she thought. After all, this was number three. Perhaps even miscarriage number four or five, because there were a couple of times when her period arrived late and clotty, her hopes dashed before she could even get a blood test.

This sucks, she thought to herself. *This totally sucks. I don't want to go through this anymore.*

The doctor had told her she could have children, and Artemis proved it was true. Their bright and athletic three-year-old little boy, who looked exactly like Armando, was a joy. But Gina wanted a son or a daughter to be a playmate for him. She didn't want to be a "one and done" as Armando called the SEALs who signed up for six years, did one tour, and then were out. Somehow, in order to be a real mother, Gina thought she needed to produce at least two or three.

Most relatives in Armando's Puerto Rican family had six or seven children. Felicia, his mother, had two who never made it to grade school. But after immigrating to the United States, she raised Armando and Mia, which fulfilled all her dreams.

Gina knew this wasn't logical. There was no such thing as being a good or a bad mother. A woman wasn't unfulfilled if she didn't have any children at all. Gina had many friends on the police force, when she was working, who chose that path. But that little creepy voice in the middle of the night whispered in her ear and shook her very soul to bits, telling her, "You're not good enough, Gina. Armando deserves better."

Maybe if she'd had a good relationship with her mother, or her father, whom she never met, things would be different. But raised by her grandmother as an only child, she figured her calling was public service. She joined the police force and decided to live in the world of men, until she got her life figured out.

She hated criminals. She didn't see them as victims at all, but as predators. Just like the predator who killed her mother.

"So why can't I just have another child, God?" she

asked the big man upstairs. "I've been good, I've prayed about it, I've even been to church, and I'm a good wife. I have a wonderful husband who loves me and would love me no matter what. But that's not enough. Why, God, is this not enough?"

She had retired—not really retiring, just quitting the police force—after a few difficult encounters with some of the higher-ups. She doubted with her five-foot-three-inch frame that she'd ever make captain or chief, though some women did. She just knew that they'd never let her in the door.

And after they got pregnant with Artemis, she believed her highest and best calling was to stay home and raise him. It was a big risk, but she didn't want to interfere with her pregnancy. She decided, Armando agreed, and that was that.

And she missed it every day.

She'd had friends that stayed on or transferred to other jurisdictions, a few out of state even. She had a good friend who went to Florida and was quite successful in her career there. Gina attended some parties and socialized at gatherings, and the question would always be asked of her... "When are you coming back?"

She knew no one would think ill of her if she did, but Artemis wasn't in school yet, only preschool. Therefore, it would be abandoning him to go back on the job.

But she needed to prove herself... if only to herself. Like she'd told Armando when they first began dating, she couldn't put her finger on why she liked the police life, but something about it stood against the naysaying voice in her head. That was the truth then. And it still was the truth today.

If she couldn't have children, she should throw herself back into public service. She could be one of the good guys in a world of crazies.

Over the next few days, she knew SEAL wives would stop by to check on her, bring food, or offer to babysit Artemis. And while she was grateful for Felicia and Gus helping, these constant visits were things she was going to have to endure, not really anything she relished. Although, she did appreciate the effort. And that was the main thing. They were trying to help her heal. Gina just knew the only thing that would heal her was if she got pregnant again and carried the baby to full term.

She recalled the unkind words she'd said to Armando, who was probably grieving just as badly as she was. It wasn't fair to him. It wasn't fair to any of them in the family.

"Am I being unfair to myself? Is it right that I should feel this way? Why do I keep obsessing about this?"

Her logical side won out. She lay back on the bed, resigned to the new day, and the new opportunities. Her heart would lighten in time. Kindness of others would rub off on her, dull the pain, and bring her back to life. She was lucky and living a blessed life, and in time, she'd learn to appreciate all of it. But for now, it was just enduring all the contact she would need to have with all those people.

"Maybe that's why I sent him away."

Armando would've stayed up all night with her, held her hand, kissed her, and told her how much he loved her. She knew this.

But she didn't want that.

She wanted a baby.

GINA CAME OUT of the shower after changing into her street clothes, preparing to be discharged. Armando hadn't shown up yet, but he had texted that he was on his way. Sitting on a chair next to her bed was Christy Lansdowne, Kyle's wife. Christy had always had the most logical and yet emotionally available mind and heart of any of the SEAL wives. She was aptly charged with caring for the families, being the liaison. While Kyle was the men's LPO, Christy was every bit the LPO of the families.

Her smile was infectious.

"Ah, there she is. You look great, Gina." Christy

lowered her forehead but still stared up at her. "I sincerely mean that, Gina. You look great."

It almost caused her to burst into tears. Instead, she quickly pretended to dab the water around her face and ears and got rid of the moisture that had accumulated in her eyes. In a whisper, she answered Christy, "Thanks."

"Now don't try to do too much, Gina, and we're going to make sure you've got meals and things. Any special requests?" she asked her.

"You mean since the last time I lost a baby? Have my taste buds changed too?" Gina immediately knew it was a mistake to say that. She closed her eyes and clenched her fists in front of her waist. "I'm so sorry."

Christy looked down at her hands wringing in her lap. "I'd like to say I understand, but you're just going to have to believe me when I say I do. You do the best you can, and we aren't going to judge anything you say. It's something that's going to take time. And you know since you've been through this before, it hurts me to say, but time heals all wounds, right?"

Christy was tiptoeing on thin ice with these comments. Gina could have let her have it, but she exerted self-control. It was unfair to hate someone, even someone so perfect as Christy Lansdowne. With her tall, thin frame, her gorgeous blonde hair, her model looks, and successful Realtor background, she made motherhood, having a career, and being married to the most respected SEAL on SEAL Team 3 look easy. And Gina knew it was anything but.

"Gina, we got news last night that one of the men on the team has fallen and is not coming back."

"Oh my gosh. You should be there. Forget about me. I'm fine. I'm healthy. That family—who is it?"

"Erik."

"The new shooter?" Gina realized this was the man who took Armando's place when he asked for family leave due to Gina's delicate condition. She couldn't fathom how she would feel if Armando had gone on the mission and not returned. Another SEAL wife out there had it much worse than she did. But even that realization didn't make her feel better.

Gina exhaled, shrugging, as if she'd given up the resistance. "I don't see how you do it, Christy. There are so many problems these days, with guys getting sick or wounded. It seems like all the places the Teams are going now have really stepped up as far as danger, and the bad guys don't seem to mind the engagement any longer. Or is that just my negative thinking?"

Christy nodded slowly, still searching her hands. "You're very astute, Gina. Kyle and I have talked about this at length. And I don't want you to tell anyone, but I'm working on him to get out. I just don't think he needs to be doing this. It's a young man's job, and I need him at home. The kids need him too. You know how it goes. Armando's nearly the same age."

Armando had been Kyle's best friend going through Bud's training and deployments. He was Kyle's go-to guy, the one whose advice he sought. And Gina knew that there was a part of going back in action that Armando missed. So while he sat beside her as she was losing the baby, he'd rather have been on a battle-field somewhere. Possibly even risking or losing his life. "Why do they do this, Christy?"

"They do it because they can. They do it because they're the guys that get it done. They do what others can't so we can live. And they make it look easy, don't they?"

It was Gina's time to nod silently.

Christy stood up and stretched her arms to the side. "Gina, let me give you a hug. I have some things I have to do before going to Sambra's house. They are expecting me to show up at Brandy and Tucker's first. There we're going to assemble some things for her. Unfortunately, we have to make more kits, more care packages. I've been so damned busy I haven't kept up on the inventory. Plus, it will be good to see everyone, have us do something as a wives' team, just like the guys do."

She checked her watch and added, "And then I'm to meet the honor team as they go over to visit Sambra.

It's a long fucking day. I've got the kids at my dad's, probably driving him crazy, but we've got work to do. I would ask you to accompany me and help, and there's nobody else I'd rather have help me but you. But I can't ask that. And it would be wrong for you to do so. Instead, just think about getting well and getting your feet back on the ground, so you can help me carry the load. I don't say this to burden you; I say this because you've still got a job to do."

Gina collapsed in her arms, sobbing.

"It never ends, does it?" Gina mumbled.

"It never does, sweetheart."

CHAPTER 3

ARMANDO HAD PLANNED to pick up Gina at 10:00. She'd driven him off the hospital grounds the night before, but he was hoping that drawing out their homecoming would soften her heart a bit. He knew she was hurting big time. He understood all of it. He didn't enjoy bearing the brunt of her nasty anger, but he did understand her. He even felt the same way.

The problem? There was no one to blame. At least in a failed mission, with a personnel dustup, or after an argument between Team guys, apologies and re-phrased instructions and feelings smoothed over the rough spots that occasionally popped up. But in this case, this was just mother nature leveling her scythe and taking no prisoners, reaping the good with the bad, the innocent with the dirty, without much thought or feeling. It just was what it was. They were dealt a bitter, brutal card. There would have to be a better day coming up, and he hoped it would be soon.

So he'd have to take her wrath until she was out of that hot wind of anger seething in her body. He decided to stop by the Team 3 building at Coronado and run the course, go for a swim, use some of the weights and the equipment, make himself an awful cup of coffee, and maybe shoot the shit with some guys that happened to be there. A lot of healing went on in that building. This time, after their last deployment to Africa, the Team was going to need more than usual. Maybe there he could help and heal himself in the process.

He wasn't looking for someone to accuse him of creating the space or the availability for Erik to go on the mission, a mission that killed him. He just wanted to rub shoulders with the combat veterans he'd been through things with and the young guys coming up the ranks who he wanted to learn to trust and show how it was done—how to be a man, how to be a hero, how to take care of the Brotherhood. He could do that, and in doing that, it would make him feel better.

Of course, being a man of action, working out always was the best solution for Armando. And it was true, in most cases, the SEALs found healing in physical exertion, more so than discussing their problems or issues or complaining. Unless it was complaining about somebody who really wasn't a good guy, a poser, or a higher up in the head shed who thought he was

Mr. God's gift to women, the teams, the president, and anyone else who would listen.

There were a few of those guys. The ones who thought they could skirt the edges, cross the lines, sometimes even abuse civilians, and get away with it. And most of the guys on SEAL Team 3 would never have anything of it. They'd gotten rid of several commissioned officers in the past, men who mistreated women, usually when they were on foreign missions, but occasionally men who hit or beat up their wives. Those men should never be put in leadership positions, Armando thought. And the team usually assisted in making it so.

But it was kind of a shit job to do.

Fredo was the first team guy he saw.

"Armani, you old fart!" the Latino SEAL said as he punched Armando's arm and then slapped his back. "I guess you heard about Erik. It's a damn shame too. He was a good kid." Fredo was not looking him in the eyes and had his little stubby fingers on his hips, shaking his head from side to side. Armando noticed that his teammate now was sporting a gold earring. He couldn't resist taking a jab at him.

"So Mia's got you dressing up. You wearing lipstick too?"

Fredo tented his eyebrows, angled his jaw, and pinched his earlobe.

Armando and Fredo were brothers-in-law, since Fredo married Armando's sister, Mia. They had more kids than they had a right to, Armando thought, yet he was grateful and thankful for them. They had a set of twins and two others, and this came after years of Fredo wondering whether or not he was sterile, thinking he was sterile. He'd even been told by a doctor that his little tadpoles had no tails. That was something no man should ever be told. But he survived and got himself healthy. Cooper convinced him to eat tofu and all kinds of extra vegetables and drink almond milk. Then, miracle of miracles, Fredo wound up growing little tails on his tadpoles.

Fredo leveled this head and squinted. "You're looking for a fight Armani?"

"Nah, just trying to give you some shit. That's all. I heard about our loss, and maybe you don't know, but I have one too."

Fredo looked up at him. "Holy shit, you don't mean Gina—"

"Yes, sir, we're 0 for 3 now."

"You mean you're 1 for 4. That's a whole lot different. You got Artemis."

"My mistake." Armando sidestepped Fredo and headed for the back of the building where the free weights were. It was dark and smelled like steel and rust and sweat. It was exactly the kind of hole he needed to be in. But that wasn't going to last very long, because he knew Fredo would take the bait.

"So you're going to go back there and sulk?" the height-challenged SEAL yelled at him. His voice echoed against the aluminum walls of the metal building. Somebody dropped a barbell on the concrete floor, someone else muttered something, and another swore under his breath. But nobody came running to Fredo's or Armando's defense.

Armando turned but still walked backwards toward the dark corner. "Okay, I'm over it now. So you want to join me or what?" Armando shouted back.

Fredo jogged to where he could walk in tandem. "You know this is why I didn't get married until I was older, Armani. I think guys who get married go ape shit, you know? They change. I knew you before. You knew me before, and look at what kind of palace dogs we've become, right?"

"I'm just venting Fredo. You know that. I don't mean anything by it."

"Maybe you ought to have Cooper come over and cook for you guys. You know it worked for me. I mean tofu is supposed to be one of the miracle foods. Spirulina, kale, all that crap. The first few sips, I hated. But after a while, I got a little used to it. Anything tastes better looking across the table at your two little kids in a high chair spilling milk everywhere. I'll put up with a little of that if I can have that family. And I'm not saying this to make you feel bad, but seriously, Armando, I know how sick they get, and maybe Gina just needs to eat some different kinds of foods?"

"It would be worth my life to try to tell her that. You want to do that?"

"Oh, hell no. I'd sooner cut off my big toe, and I'm kind of fond of my big toe on account that it keeps me from tipping over when I'm running."

"Then shut the fuck up. Let's not talk about foods, food groups, babies, or pregnant women. Let's not even talk about women at all. Why don't you tell me what went down on the team? I need to know, because Gina's going to ask me."

Armando saw the change in Fredo's expression. A deadly scowl covered his lower face.

"He was getting in position. He came down to get another scope, because I guess either the one you used wasn't there or it was broken or something. I don't know what it was, but he had to sneak down and get another scope. TJ happened to have one, and so he took it back to the perch and got ready. Before he could get settled in there was some action down in the compound, and he took a look through the scope to see if he could get a bead on anyone and somebody blasted him right here." Fredo showed Armando with his forefinger balanced perfectly in the middle of his forehead.

"God, that's cold. He probably never knew it happened." Armando stared at his feet.

"That's a fact, Armani. I saw his face when we got him down out of the tree, and the fucker was still smiling. God knows what he was thinking, but it was the last thing he heard or saw or felt. He sure didn't hear or see the round that hit him. I guess if you have to go, that would be the way to go."

Armando wasn't excited about talking about bullets to the brain, because his level of despair had bordered on that territory. If it wasn't for Gina and little Artemis, he really wouldn't have had much to live for. He chalked it up to being something from his dark somber side, something that luckily never got to surface, because he became a Navy SEAL instead. He chose becoming a hero instead of a bad guy. But he could have gone either way.

The team building was being underused today, and Armando knew it was probably one of those days when guys would stay home, hug their wives and kids, and just hole in for a bit. That was often what they did when they got home from a difficult deployment. So he was grateful to have met up with Fredo.

On the way over to the hospital to pick up Gina, he gave Kyle a call.

"Sure good to be back in San Diego. You get filled

in by anyone yet?" Kyle asked.

"I spoke a little bit with Fredo. That's a damn shame. My number two scope was in the bag when I handed it over, but who knows, someone could have messed with it. Sorry about that, Kyle."

"Nobody's blaming you. He should have had it ready before. You know that. Check your equipment first, twice, and three times more. That's why we don't wait to get set up. He didn't check. That's on him."

Armando knew he was going to ask about Gina so he brought it up first. "I'm on my way over to pick Gina up now. She got a little testy with me last night. I admit, perhaps I wasn't what she needed. But she's going to be okay, physically. I think it's going to take some time for her, and I was wondering if maybe we could apply for more family leave under the circumstances."

Kyle's sigh was long and raspy. "Depends on what comes down the line." Armando could imagine the shrug folding Kyle's shoulders just from the sound of his voice. "You know I don't control that at all. They may ask for a shooter for something else. They may TDR a handful of you guys. It really depends. But if I can, I'll get it for you, Armando."

"Thanks, man. Anything you can do."

Armando gave Kyle a brief description of how things had gone, and that the doctor had mentioned that there shouldn't be anything that would keep Gina from having healthy children in the future.

"That's good. That's real good. You just keep thinking about that," Kyle said.

Armando didn't have any response to that, and it was all he could do to stop from mumbling like an idiot. He was going to sign off because the drawn-out pause was just too damn awkward. He didn't know what to tell his LPO. He was hesitant to talk about some of the things bouncing around his brain. So he waited to be asked.

He didn't have to wait long.

"So, Armani, you're going to have to figure out what it is you're going to do. You're need to check out your priorities a bit. You got little Artemis. If Gina doesn't bounce back right away, you're going to be like a single parent for a while. Which is fine. But if you get called up, and you don't go, well, you've missed a lot of group time. I don't think Watkins or any of those guys are going to like it at all. It could affect your career."

Armando didn't have to see his own face in the rearview mirror. He knew he'd find tears there. But he buried everything as deep as he could and just answered with a simple, "Roger that. I won't forget. I won't let you down." His voice was raspy so he coughed his way to finishing his sentence.

"Christy's going over to Erik's house with the Honor Guard. I think she stopped by to see Gina on her way. You might see her when you get there."

"Good on her. Man, that gal's busy."

"You could say that again. Sometimes I think she works harder than I do. And these days it seems like we've got so many people hurt, things happening, dumb stuff too. We got families with money problems and divorces and kids running away or getting caught up in the law. Some days, I think like I'm running a zoo, not a SEAL team."

"Have you ever thought about getting out, Kyle?"

"Not really."

The answer was too quick. Armando knew from the tone of his voice that he was lying. So he continued. "You know, I'm going to evaluate everything carefully. I need to see what Gina wants to do. If she says she wants to move somewhere and go do something else, I think I'm going to let that affect my decision to stay on the teams or not. But hell, Kyle, we're not getting any younger. And it just seems to be getting tougher and tougher. You sense the same?"

"Yup. I think about that every day. And you never heard that from me."

"No, I never did."

"But just be careful, give it lots of thought. Maybe you guys should go see Dr. Brownlee—get some perspective on this whole thing."

"Gina hates shrinks."

"And that's probably exactly why she should go. Besides Brownlee is a friend, right?"

"Like family, Kyle. I think he knows more about the team than you do."

"You can roger that. So promise me this, Armando, before you make any stupid decisions or get in a huge argument with your wife, promise me you'll go get some help. If it's not Brownlee, somebody good. And I can give you a list if you want. But I want you to talk to somebody. I don't want the two of you to decide your future without pulling somebody else in who isn't on the team but is a team loyalist. You know what I mean."

Dr. Brownlee was Cooper's father-in-law, a very noted and renowned psychiatrist in the San Diego area, who had seen and dealt with many of the SEALs on Team 3 over the years. They had parties and get-togethers at the Brownlee home, especially during the happier days when Mrs. Brownlee was alive. But that didn't negate the fact that the Brownlees were part of their support team.

"I hear you, Kyle. And I'll do it. I promise."

CHAPTER 4

G INA SAT ON the hospital bed as Armando breezed through the doorway. The sight of his handsome face did make her heart skip a beat, and her chest welled up with pride that this good man had chosen her for a life partner. She'd never thought she could meet a man so wonderful. She'd never expected it.

But here he was. Handsome and tall, his dark features, including riveting brown eyes and shiny black hair, melted her insides as he stared down at her. Then his face exploded in a warm smile. It was all for her. It came straight from his heart, she knew that for sure.

"Great to see you, sweetheart," he said.

"Armando—"

He cut her off. "Gina, you don't have to explain anything. You can yell at me as much as you like, and I'm not going to leave. I just gave you some space, and I'll give you as much time as you need. But you're not going to have to worry about me going away. I'm here for the long haul. I'm here no matter how many kids we have, no matter what happens. I'm here for you and for Artemis. I just want you to know that."

"But it still wasn't right. And I'm so sorry. I had no right to treat you that way."

"You do the best you can, and I'll be here to pick up the pieces, if there are any. You just take care of you. Don't worry about me. I got this. Remember that, Gina."

He raced to the bed, picked her up in his arms, and held her tight against his body. The feeling was warm as he infused strength into her body just by the way his muscles tightened around her torso. He could have squeezed the life out of her, and she wouldn't have minded. She belonged to him in every sense of the word.

As he released her and she got her bearings, which was a struggle since she was swooning all over the place, she picked up her overnight bag and slung it over her shoulder. Holding one hand with him, they exited the room together.

At the floor desk, they both signed the discharge papers, and a wheelchair was provided for her. Armando gripped the handles and asked her to sit.

"Absolutely no way. I can walk out on my own. I'm not an invalid."

"No can do, Gina. It's hospital rules. You got to

leave the hospital in a wheelchair. What you do when you get in the car is your business," the heavy-set charge nurse told her. She made a copy of several instruction sheets and then handed them to Armando. "These are what the doctor's orders are."

Gina sat in the metal contraption with "Labor and Delivery" spray-painted on the back and allowed her husband to push her with one hand. His other hand rested on her shoulder and sometimes eased over to the back of her neck to give it a squeeze. It was so comforting to have him be there with her, and she knew her emotions were on edge. Every time he touched her, she felt hot tears gather on her lower eyelids.

After they headed down the elevator and toward the ground floor pickup area, Armando helped her into their car, and the orderly who had followed them down took the wheelchair back inside. Armando sat in the driver's seat, made sure her seatbelt was fastened, and asked, "You want a cappuccino, some decent breakfast, or what? I'm open for anything. I could eat breakfast; I could drink a coffee; I could walk on the beach with you. As long as it's with you, Gina, anything you want. Just tell me."

He leaned over and planted a kiss on her forehead.

Gina finally let the tears fall. Armando just sat there waiting, his right hand in both of hers before he started the car and headed out of the parking lot.

"Which way?"

"Left. Let's go to the beach, down by the Hotel Del?"

"Sweetheart, I'm going to do anything you want, but that's about forty minutes away, you know that. Are you sure you're open to a long drive? Some of that's going to be on the freeway with traffic, too."

"I want *that* beach. A place where you guys used to train. I want to go there please."

"All right. The lady says the beach, so the beach it is."

She passed all the places that were so familiar to her now, all the little restaurants and coffee houses, the dress shops she frequented, even the maternity shop she started to buy clothes from. She passed the ice cream shops, the sandal stores, and a couple of their favorite hangouts with some of the Team guys. They even passed by The Scupper, where a few young new Tadpoles or wannabes were sitting out on the patio under the umbrella, having fun and ogling the buxom waitress who was trying to serve them beers before noon. Everything was so normal here. Everything hadn't been affected by their tragedy. Life went on. Gina was struck with that.

It wasn't fair that life had to go on, even though she still felt that she had failed. She was going to have to work at that. She knew she was going to have to purge that thought from her mind. She decided now was as good a time as any to begin giving him some of her thoughts about the future.

"Sweetheart, I've been thinking about some things." She turned to see how Armando reacted to the statement.

"And?" His sexy smile warmed her body.

"I feel like I've been waiting these past few years, waiting to get pregnant again. And we've gone through this so many times now. Maybe it's time to stop. Maybe we should just be happy with one child. And I know you told me several times already, but you know I'm not built that way. I just can't face the possibility of this happening again. I really want more children, Armando, but I just don't want to look at your face again if we lose another. Maybe God is telling me that Artemis needs to be our whole life."

"Honey, I think that's very wise. You take some time, and I'll do whatever you want. It's your decision 100%. If you change your mind and you decide you want to try again, I'm here for you. I'm here for us, for whatever is ahead of us. But you have to make that decision. My job is to make it work. To the extent that I can." He wrinkled his eyebrow slightly, and Gina could tell he wasn't happy with that last sentence.

She was proud she didn't let that bother her.

"I know what you mean, Armando, and it's going to take me a while to not feel guilty. I probably always will. That's just going to have to be something I bear."

"Gina, the logic of it is that it isn't your fault. It's genetics. It's environmental factors. It's stress. It's—"

"But I'm not on the job any more. I don't have any stress. All I do is take care of Artemis. I volunteer, and I help my sisters on the teams, but other than taking care of you and Artemis, I don't work anymore. And I've been thinking maybe I should. Maybe I should consider going back."

Armando turned and stared at her without expression. "You don't mean that, do you?"

She could see by the tiny outline of a worried brow that he was concerned.

"Yeah, I'm considering it. I called the station. I talked to our old union rep, and she said they've got lots of vacancies. She said, at first, I wouldn't be able to get anything like what I did before, but she could set it up so that I added to my pension."

Armando interrupted her this time. "No, Gina, I would not be in favor of you doing that again. Undercover work, while exciting, is for young single women without families."

"Like the Teams?" She resisted him.

Armando nodded solemnly. As he pulled into the Hotel Del parking lot, which, as usual, was overpacked with tourists, he took a deep breath and then blew it out. "Yes. It is just like the teams. But I can't for the life of me understand why Artemis should have both parents who are putting themselves in harm's way. I mean—"

"Don't you think I can handle it? We were together when I did it before."

"But that was before we had Artemis, honey," he protested.

She crossed her arms in front of her chest, staring out over her right shoulder at the people winding their way through the parking lot to the restaurant or hotel.

"I'm saying that I'm not sure that's a wise decision, but if you say that's what you want to do, I'll go with it. I'm just not happy seeing you do something dangerous, risky. Not homicide, not undercover. A desk job. Paperwork. Traffic Division."

"Armando, you know traffic cops get into trouble all the time. Traffic stops are getting to be one of the most dangerous things cops on the beat can do. I could get killed just crossing the street or walking into a convenience store and having my gun stolen and pulled on me. Stopping a robbery? Responding to a domestic dispute? They're all dangerous now. You know that."

"So maybe you ease into something like that. Maybe you go for some kind of desk duty first. They might want to test your mettle first too, Gina, since it's been—what?—six years?"

"Five years and eight and a half months. You want to know how many days?"

"No, thanks. I got the message."

Gina could see he was not happy.

ARTEMIS PUSHED HIS way through the front door with his grandparents right behind. He made a beeline for Gina.

"Mommy! Mommy! Grandma and Grandpa say they're going to buy me a puppy, if you say it's okay. Please, please, please can I have a puppy?"

Gina allowed the smell of her young, precocious three-year-old to completely envelope her. His hair was freshly shampooed and smelled like the brand of baby shampoo she still used on him, even though he was well beyond the baby stage. She felt his chubby little body, all the soft fatty portions of the back of his arms, the backs of his thighs, and how his chest caved into hers as his tiny rapid heartbeat thumped against hers. He was such a joy, and her tears were not sad ones, but tears of rejoicing for this beautiful little boy, the miracle, of Artemis.

She held him at arm's length finally to give him a good look over. "I can see your grandma and grandpa managed to put about five pounds on you in just twenty-four hours. What have you been eating, Artemis?"

"Pancakes. Cupcakes. Chicken nuggets. I got some alphabet soup too. I ate very well, Mama."

Gina hugged him again and relished the feel of his chubby arms gripping her neck. It made her feel joy having him there too, just like his father did. She looked up at Gus and Felicia. "Thanks so much, guys. I can see I'm going to have to undo all those appetites he's come over with."

Former San Diego Police Sergeant Gus Mayfield, her stepfather-in-law, started announcing in his rough tone, "Oh damn, Gina, pancakes aren't bad for anybody. The more syrup and butter on them the better. And the way Felicia makes them with raspberries and strawberries and whipped cream—"

"Yes, Mama, whipped cream! Do you have some? I want whipped cream on my hot chocolate and on my pancakes and on my fruits." Artemis was insistent.

Gus Mayfield shrugged and held his hands out to the side, powerless against the women in his life that he loved and his little step-grandson. He knew he was going to lose the battle, but he tried anyway.

"Artemis, son, I think your mom is going to overrule us on this. But don't you give up. Next time you guys come over to our place, I'll make sure you get your whipped cream, okay? Is that a deal?"

Artemis extracted himself from Gina's lap, went over, and offered Gus Mayfield a high five as far as he could reach above his head. "Deal."

They slapped hands, and then Artemis ran to his father and hugged him about the knees.

Armando was overjoyed with the attention. "I think your mama's right, but you know I'm way more lenient with you than your mama is, so maybe we'll work it out sometime." Armando winked at Gina. "Maybe you and I will go to a pancake house or something, where mama won't see. Would you like that?"

"Yes, please." Artemis started skipping around the living room looking for toys and things that he could consume himself with.

Armando gave him a little direction. "Why don't you go on back to your bedroom and see if you can show Grandma and Grandpa your new Lego set that we got you the other day. Would you like that?" Armando asked him. Without saying a word, Artemis disappeared to the back of the house.

Gina stood up and gave Felicia and Gus a hug. Her Puerto Rican mother-in-law smelled like fried foods, cooking breads, all kinds of things that she miraculously baked and made from scratch. Her hair was neatly tied in a braid which wrapped around the top of her head. She wore a dress she'd gotten in Mexico on one of their vacations. It suited her, with brightly colored flowers covering the upper smock of her neck and shoulders. The dress was white, but the decorations were every color of the rainbow. It looked like Felicia's garden, which was also brightly colored with the largest dahlias and roses Gina had ever seen. This woman, who had undergone great hardship, had a fondness for children. She was a terrific cook, mother, and grandmother, and she had a green thumb unlike anyone she'd ever met. She was all heart, all woman, and strong as hell.

"Thank you, Mom."

"Oh, come on. We love to have him over. Sometime, you must go somewhere on vacation and leave Artemis with us for a week, maybe two? We'd love to have him."

"Yes, we're buying a new RV, so maybe we could take him camping?" Gus Mayfield added.

"You guys are going to be campers, RVers?" Armando asked.

"Yes, we went to one of those big shows last weekend. I didn't tell you with all of this stuff going on—" Gus was embarrassed by bringing up Gina's hospital stay, but he continued anyway. "We put a deposit down on something, and it'll be ready in about a month. It's a 26-footer, brand new, tow trailer, and it's awesome. It's got everything in it including an outdoor kitchen, and it's got a big screen TV, even on the outside."

"He can watch sports at the beach instead of watching the beach. Or he can take it while he's fishing. He has to have his TV when he's doing anything these days," said Felicia.

"That sounds nice," Armando said. "We'll see if we can take you up on that. I'm sure Artemis would love it."

"Maybe we could take a trip up north sometime, Armando? You know, go see Zak and the wineries up there. It's been years now," Gina mentioned.

Armando nodded. "It was one of the weddings, maybe Jameson's. I think that was the last time we were up there. Too long. We ought to do that, Gina. I think that's just what the doctor ordered."

As he smiled to her, Gina began to feel her world come back to life.

"So it's settled then," Felicia said. "You pick the time, and after we get the motor home, we'll take him camping, and you guys go have some fun. Go see your friends and get out of here."

CHAPTER 5

I N THE WEEKS that passed, following Gina's miscarriage, Armando threw himself into some extra
team duties, taking several marksman trainings with a
couple of his Marine sniper friends who we were
visiting from Fayetteville. He even enrolled in a com-
petitive shoot-out and nearly took home the trophy.

The whole Team used more ammo in one week of
practice than many Marine and Army units did in an
entire year. But he bettered that. In three weeks, and he
marked it all down carefully, he'd shot more practice
rounds than he had done the previous year—all twelve
months. But then, the shooters on any SEAL Team
were often doing that.

He found a calm level spot in the middle of his
heart, even though he witnessed Gina's fight to stay
positive. She showered Artemis with affection and
attention, which seemed to help her mood. Armando
was hopeful, despite knowing she was struggling.

Born under some lucky star, Artemis seemed unaffected by all the family drama. Armando was grateful for that.

But their sex life was nonexistent.

He began thinking that perhaps he was the cause of her miscarriage. In his selfish need to have sex, he'd caused her pain and anguish. Or she somehow got the message that he wouldn't want her if she didn't produce another child for him. But nothing could be further from the truth. This produced an angry burr under his saddle, and it bothered him nearly 24/7.

Unlike prior negative situations, this one was more difficult to bounce back from, mostly because it had such a horrible effect on Gina.

The funeral for Erik had been very moving. It had been a clear, early summer morning, overlooking the inlet they'd trained in. The ships passed back and forth in the murky waters of the San Diego harbor. All of the Team guys who were in town were there, as well as many of the parents, sisters, and brothers. He didn't really want Gina to attend, but she insisted. And he knew it was so she could show the rest of the team she was well.

But she was far from well. He knew it. She knew it.

Although he had urged her to come to couple's therapy, she was hesitant to do anything other than what she was doing. He began to feel that she was stuck in place and perhaps they were going to be months—maybe even years—in the recovery process.

He also told himself whatever it took, however long it took, he was there for her. He wasn't going to intervene harshly or try her make her do something she didn't want to. He just needed to let her know she had his full support.

He took it upon himself to bring Gina out to restaurants and places that they used to frequent before, making sure she understood how important he felt being around her was. She'd made it to the funeral, but they couldn't quite take in the gathering afterwards. Subsequently, she also abstained from attending any other SEAL functions, such as bonfires or birthday parties or other celebrations.

He was okay with that.

He recalled how she looked at the funeral—how she'd stared at Erik's coffin. When they all placed their Tridents on the casket, the wives jumped at the sound of their little symbol of bravery being pounded one by one into the casket lid. It was as loud and as forceful as a 21-gun salute. They had done it so many times, yet each one was special for him, and each time, he grieved for not only this fallen warrior but for all the ones who came before.

Sambra, Erik's widow, would not make eye contact with him. He guessed what the source of that could be.

After all, Erik probably told her that the reason for his deployment was because Armando was at home with Gina. And it wasn't Armando's place to change whatever she'd been told. But what he thought strange was how Sambra stared at Gina. Did she even know what had befallen Gina? Had they had a disagreement, something he hadn't seen?

Of all the people in the audience, Sambra only focused on Gina. She didn't focus on Erik's parents, who had flown down from Oregon, or Kyle or Christy or any of the members of the team who had assisted him, included him in their brotherhood. It was only Gina she was interested in. And that seemed very strange.

But as the weeks passed and his trainings were behind him, he began regularly taking Gina out to dinner again, just like they'd done when they were first married. He had no idea if it was working, but it was the only thing he could think to do. The two of them never talked about Erik's death or what their future was. The void between them appeared to be permanent.

He hoped it would change soon.

On one of their evenings together, Gina spoke up and said something to him he thought he'd never hear from her lips.

"Armando, do you think it would be best if we separated?"

He stared into her completely expressionless face, a woman he now was beginning to feel he didn't know at all.

"Where in the hell did that come from?"

"Well, it's just that you and I hardly talk. We don't have much to say to one another. We do take care of Artemis, but it's like—I don't know—I feel like I'm dead to you."

"I haven't wanted to push you, Gina. I figured I would give you the space you asked for. Remember, you asked to have some space, some time by yourself. I'm trying to give you that, honey."

She blankly stared at her unfinished dinner. "Well, I still think I'd like a separation. I've thought about it a lot, and I think that's what I need right now."

Armando was starting to sweat, his heart in a near panic over these strange words.

"Gina, I don't understand. We were about to plan a trip up north to the wine country. This is the first time I've ever heard of this, and I need to know where it's coming from. Why have you suddenly decided this is something you want?"

"I thought it would be something *you* wanted. Because you don't want me."

"I never said that, Gina. I've never once told you that."

"You look at me, and you feel sad. I see it in your

face. I don't like to be the person who makes you sad. No woman wants to be the reason her man is unhappy. Women want to inspire their husbands, not pull them down into their own pits of hell."

"This is crazy nonsense you're talking here. I don't feel that way at all. The only thing I've ever said to you—and I sincerely mean it, sweetheart—is that I am not going anywhere. I'm here. I'm here for as little or as long as you want me."

"Well, maybe I don't want this anymore."

Again, she wasn't smiling. She looked straight into his eyes and didn't show him an ounce of warmth. Armando felt as if all the blood had left his body.

"This completely floors me, sweetheart. I don't feel that way about you, and I've never even thought that way. I don't consider that a valid solution. I mean, of all the things that we could do, separating seems like the least effective thing for us to solve whatever's going on between us. What happened with this baby is neither of our faults."

"Are you sure?"

"Absolutely. And while we're on the subject, you agreed that at some point we should start seeing a counselor. I really need that now, especially with these words you're giving me. I need us to talk to somebody who's more equipped to handle our issues, give us better advice. Do you see that now, sweetheart?"

She leaned back in her chair and set her fork down on top of her napkin, staring at her unfinished food. She took a long sip of water and then gathered her purse. Looking up at Armando, she said, "I want to go home."

It was a long ride to the house, and neither one of them said a word. Armando's mind raced over what could have happened, how she could have arrived at this conclusion. There was something he'd missed. Did she have a conversation with someone that threw her off-kilter? Or was she just coming from the space of being confused. And he could understand that. God, in the fog of war, he was confused all the time. This was like war for her. Didn't make it any easier on him, but it was definitely a battle for Gina. He was outmatched by the depth of her despair.

They pulled up into the driveway, and before exiting the car, he posed a question to her. "Before we talk anymore about this, or not talk about it, or whatever it is that's going on… Before we may make any decisions, I'm going to insist that we see a counselor. I don't want to have another day go by without getting some help here. I feel like I'm way out of my league. I try to be gentle with you. I try to give you space. I try to engage you by taking you out to dinners. I encourage you to be social, and I support you when you don't want to be. I can't think of anything I've done that would make you want to be alone by yourself. Gina—" He reached for her hand, and she let him take it in both of his. "Gina, I love you. I want what's best for us, and if I thought doing a separation was the best, easiest, or fastest way for us to get back on track, I'd be the first one to cheer for it. But that's not what this is. This is giving up. And I'm not willing to. You're worth fighting for, Gina."

She stared down at her hand between his and then softly added, "Okay. I'll set something up for tomorrow. I don't want to use Dr. Brownlee or anybody on the base. I'd like to use somebody private, if we could."

"You set it up, sweetheart. And I'll be there."

After Armando came back from taking the babysitter home, he suggested she go to bed early and told her that he would sleep with Artemis in his bedroom. She gave no objection. In the middle of the night, he heard her sobbing through the thin walls of their bungalow.

And he felt powerless to do anything about it. But God, how he wished he could.

THEY SAT IN the waiting room of an attractive Victorian near the strand, with the three name placards on a sign in front. It was a very trendy area, and the Victorian was brightly painted. They were let in to the counselor's office. Armando thought the young woman who helped them was the office receptionist, but she turned out to be the counselor herself. She didn't appear to be much older than fresh out of college.

"Good morning. My name is Fiona. Please have a seat where you are most comfortable." She motioned to a couch on one side and a loveseat facing it at a forty-five-degree angle on the other. Gina took the end of the loveseat, and Armando took the end of the couch to give her space.

The counselor opened brightly and asked a few ice-breaking questions. But their lack of response and hesitancy to engage in conversation caused her to change course. Armando noticed she was gathering herself to come at them full tilt. There would be no more "chitchat" today.

"So why are we here together?" she asked.

Armando turned to Gina. "You first."

After several seconds, she stared into her lap and then spoke directly to the young counselor.

"I think we want to discuss a separation. Not a permanent divorce, but a separation, a timeout. I think we both need some space."

The counselor motioned to Armando. "Mr. Guzman—may I call you Armando?" At his nod, she continued, "How does that statement make you feel?"

He was going to blurt out that it made him feel like shit, but he didn't dare do that. He decided to play it careful, so he didn't get hit with something unexpected.

The way Gina had been acting lately, he was almost beginning to expect the unexpected.

"Well, this is all new to me, since she sprung it on me last night at dinner. I didn't realize that's how she felt."

The counselor looked encouragingly at his wife. "Mrs. Guzman, may I call you Gina?" At her assent, the counselor continued. "Can you tell us more about your request?"

"I just think it's for the best." Gina continued to not make any eye contact.

The counselor glanced between the two of them and delicately posed another question to Gina. "So you've been thinking about this for some time, or is this something you just thought of last night?" she asked Gina.

"I've been thinking about it ever since we left the hospital, about three, four weeks ago. I'm thinking that all we're doing is making each other miserable. And it's obvious we're trying too hard to be together."

"Armando? What do you have to say about that?"

Armando leaned back and searched the ceiling fan sitting idle in the center, watched the way the patterns of the leaves fell on the wall through the clearstory window that bordered the street outside. He thought about all the happy days, the good times, the fun they'd had raising Artemis, and their combined hopes for his future. Yes, there were the miscarriages, but he knew they didn't affect him as much as they affected Gina. He didn't quite know if he should tell her this or not. But he decided to do the best he could.

"I don't say this to want to make myself right or anything, but I've been wanting to spend time with a counselor for weeks now. So I'm glad we're here. It's a good first step. And I just don't want to go through any big change right now with Gina, our family life, something semi-permanent, something as large as separating, having Artemis live part-time with me and part-time with her, something like that, something so obvious and public, without us getting a firm handle on why we're doing this. And I'm going to tell you, I have no freaking idea where she's coming from on this. I'd like to know. I care about her, but for some reason, she thinks that I don't. I do! Nothing is the same without Gina. I have always loved her. I have continued to love her, and I will love her even if she desires to leave me. But I do not willingly want to separate."

He flicked a tear from his right eye and rolled his left shoulder almost as a reflex to indicate he didn't give a shit whether anybody saw that he was crying. It hurt that bad. And he was going to stop covering it up. He wanted to save his marriage.

"Gina, I'd like to hear your reasoning. I know you think you are just making each other sad, but is there anything else causing you to feel this way? Help Armando understand where you are emotionally."

"Well, like I told him last night, every woman wants to be an inspiration for her man. We have no sex life, and we hardly touch. We are like two strangers living in the same house, being very cordial, but it's BS. It hurts too much to try."

"Who does it hurt, Gina?" the counselor asked.

"Well, it hurts me. I think it hurts Artemis. And it has to hurt—"

"How does it hurt Artemis?" Armando interrupted.

"Because he's asked me what's wrong with Daddy."

"Armando, can you think of any reason why your son would ask that question?" the young counselor asked.

"I haven't a clue." He gave Gina a squinting stare. "Are you sure?"

"Are you accusing me of lying, Armando?"

"Of course not. But I just don't understand."

"Will you stop fucking saying that? Armando, open your eyes and ears. You're this Boy Scout running around doing all this shit, and you're not even paying any attention to what's going on under your own roof. Don't you see him? He's quieter. He's more reserved. He's scared of you."

Armando did not agree in the slightest. And he told them so. His anger was starting to unleash. He didn't want that to happen.

"Wait a minute, you two," the counselor interrupted. "Let's not escalate this, and let's try to keep it between the lines. Communication is important, but we cannot keep those lines open if we attack one another. It's important that we understand and respect each other's feelings."

Armando forged ahead, not listening. "Gina, you got somebody else you would rather spend the rest of your life with? Is that what it is? You've fallen out of love with me? Perhaps found somebody else?"

Gina stood, rage racking her whole body. "Goddamn you, Armando. I have sat by while you came home bloodied, sometimes wounded, almost killed from these missions. I've seen you counsel wives and children of men who have died. I've seen you jump at Kyle's beck and call and run over to somebody else's house to help handle a situation. And because I don't complain, I get ignored. I'm totally ignored. You say you love me, and I believe you. But it's not enough. I think you're masking that we are not compatible."

"What about telling you I'm not quitting, I'm staying here, I'm never going to leave your side? What about that shows I don't care about you?"

The counselor inserted herself. "Gina, thank you for your honesty in expressing how you feel. Please sit down so we can talk about this. Armando, she feels like your attention is turned from her toward your duties and your career. Can you tell her why you want to be with her?"

"Because I love you!" Armando said to Gina. "You are the love of my life, the woman I hoped to meet. I never expected to find somebody so compatible for me, so beautiful, so compassionate, so strong. I've loved you ever since our first date. And I hope you can remember what that was all about."

"Oh, you mean the hookup in the pickup truck?"

"That was special—"

"Just a minute, guys." The counselor inserted herself again. "You say hookup, Gina. Armando, you say it's special. Why don't we try to find words that you both agree with?"

She let that statement dangle in the air, and it really did feel like a fishhook in his throat. Armando fisted and unfisted his hands. Then he pounded the side of the couch arm.

"Dammit all to hell. Why don't you two figure it out, and then you let me know? I'm going to wait outside in the waiting room, and I'll let you two ladies figure out the whole fucking world. Because apparently, while I was out there killing myself, getting my ass kicked, and my brains knocked about, sacrificing myself because I want to be that guy that gets it done, you decided I wasn't good enough for you. So I'd like you to settle in and tell the truth to yourself, Gina. I'm not good enough for you. It's not the other way around. You're really accusing me of being less than the man I am. And I won't sit here and listen to it. It doesn't matter what kind of nice words you say, it's bullshit!"

CHAPTER 6

CHRISTY ASKED FOR Gina's help in distributing a meal to Erik's widow, Sambra. She apologized for asking, but she'd had someone cancel on her, and she was still trying to get a babysitter for a school event she and Kyle had to attend that evening. Gina was happy to help out, dropped Artemis off at Felicia's, texted Armando to pick him up, and then headed to Christy's house over by the beach.

Before Gina could get out of the car, she nearly ran into Brandy Hudson, Tucker's wife, who had the three Lansdowne children in tow.

"Hi. Bye," Brandy said with a wave as she helped the kids meander the walkway down to her SUV. After opening the second door, she turned and shouted over her shoulder, "I'm sorry, Gina. I wish I could stay, but we're already late for something else. I promise I'll stop by and see you soon, okay?"

Gina laughed and shook her head. "No problem,

Brandy. I'm doing fine."

She watched the young bride of the popular Navy SEAL the guys called Shrek—because of his 5XL size—load the kids in. Her husband was one of the most dedicated and decorated SEALs in Kyle's platoon. Armando respected him almost as much as he respected Kyle. With the efficiency Brandy used to wrangle the kids, some of that must have rubbed off on her.

She knocked on Christy's front door and found her putting her earrings on as she answered. "Oh, thank God. Gina, you're really helping me out of a jam here."

"I could have taken the kids. All you have to do was ask."

"You're such a dear. I know it. It's just that Brandy's so close by, and well, she owes me a couple. I've been doing some babysitting for them lately, mostly because the kids enjoy spending time together, but she was happy to take them. They've got some kind of a carnival or something coming up, so Tucker's meeting them down at the fairgrounds."

"Well, anytime. You just give the word. Now where's this dinner? If it takes any longer, I'm going to sit and eat it myself."

"You didn't have any dinner?"

"No, I dropped Artemis off at Felicia's, so—"

"Oh my God. We've got kids being shuttled all over town, don't we? Did you ever think life would get so complicated?" Christy said as she dashed down the hall to her bedroom and disappeared. She yelled for Gina to come down and see her.

The room was torn apart, and it looked like she'd ripped all three kids out of bed from taking a nap or watching TV in their room. Pillows were all over the place, the bedspread was mostly on the ground, and there was a can of Coke and a bag of potato chips propped on the headboard.

"Don't pay any attention to this. The kids, I just needed to keep them quiet so I could get ready."

"Where's Kyle?" Gina asked.

"Oh, he's got something he's doing down there at the Team building. I'm afraid this one's going to be solo. But I'm hoping. He said he'd make it. But you know these back-to-school nights are kind of boring, and if it were a teacher conference, well, he'd be there for sure. I mean, the whole place could be blowing up and he'd attend a teacher conference. You know how he is about those things."

"Indeed I do. Armando's the same way. I'm bracing myself for when Artemis attends kindergarten."

Christy changed her dress again, adding the dress to the pile already lying across the bed.

"I just can't decide what to wear. I want to look nice, but I don't want to look like somebody's grandmother, you get what I mean?"

"Christy, you would look gorgeous in anything. You could wear pajamas and no one would care."

"Well, if you say so. But I have a feeling some of the teachers would object. They always hold us kind of suspect, don't they?"

Gina shrugged her shoulders. "I'm not sure about any of that. You have way more interaction with the teachers and the schools and the other parents than I do. But trust me on this, Christy, nobody would think you were underdressed if you wore your pajamas. Honest."

Christy zipped herself up, jumped to her feet, ran over to Gina, and gave her a big hug, almost dropping them both to the bed. "I have missed you so much, Gina. I hope we can start seeing a lot more of each other now. I've just been so worried, and I just haven't known what to do. Plus, I've been so damn busy."

"It's all good, Christy. Honest." Christy gave her an odd look as if Armando had said something to Kyle that Christy was privy to. And she suspected Christy didn't believe her.

GINA STARED DOWN at the little piece of paper with Sambra's address written on it. She put it into her GPS and laid the note on top of the tinfoil covering the tuna casserole Christy had made. The casserole smelled divine. Thinking back on the day, Gina realized she just had a couple of boiled eggs for breakfast, skipped lunch, and now was really hungry for dinner.

It was a thirty-minute ride over to the other part of town, a nice little neighborhood that Gina was not familiar with. It was not the beachy scene like Coronado was, but it was a cute little subdivision of homes built around the '50s and '60s. Most of them had single-car garages. It was a very desirable area, but everything in the subdivision was small. Occasionally, she drove past a huge monstrosity of a home built on a postage-stamp-sized lot, where people had torn down the original bungalow and built McMansions on top. She imagined that was the direction the whole neighborhood was going.

But the house where Erik's widow lived was just a plain little box, probably not bigger than a two bedroom, with older windows, a nice little meandering walkway up to the front porch, green shrubs, and a lawn that needed some fertilizer and care to make it look crisp again. Some roses to the left of the front porch had bloomed a month or two before and had never been dead-headed. Gina knew from watching Felicia tend to her flowers that the roses would do much better with a little more water, a lot of fertilizer, and a severe pruning. If someone cut off the old dead flowers, two or three would bloom in their place. Maybe someday she would offer to show Sambra or bring Felicia over to help her with her garden. Right now, Gina knew that would be a terrible idea.

She brought the casserole with her. Christy had packed it with a couple of tea towels in a short box lid so that it wouldn't slide around the car. She held it gingerly and could smell the wonderful tuna flavor coming from under the tinfoil.

She only had to knock once. The door whisked opened so quickly it almost made her take a step back. What she saw on the other side of the doorway surprised her.

Sambra had pulled her hair back up into a ponytail at the top of her head, her long black hair cascading down her back. She was also wearing very heavy black eye makeup, and some of it was smudged as if she'd been crying. She had on bright orange lipstick and bright orange nail polish to match, very, very tight stretchy exercise leggings, and a big top made from an old t-shirt that had been cut and then edged with lace, like so many of the trendy fashions were these days. She was either on her way out to exercise or was just trying to be comfortable. But Gina wondered if perhaps she was getting ready to entertain someone. And not a friend either.

"Oh!" Sambra squeaked. "I didn't expect you."

Gina was hesitant and found Sambra's appearance a little disarming. "I'm sorry if you didn't realize I was bringing this over. And I'm Gina, by the way. I met you for the first time at the funeral."

"I know exactly who you are," Sambra answered.

"Well, I'm sure you've been getting meals and things from the other wives, and tonight, it's my turn, although I didn't make this, and you're kind of lucky I didn't. Christy did. It's her world-famous tuna casserole. And I'll tell you what, I have eaten this probably ten times, and I never tire of it. So you're in for a treat."

Sambra looked down at the casserole and then stared at Gina's eyes. She reached for the cardboard box, stepped back behind her, and invited Gina in. As Gina followed behind her all the way to the kitchen, Sambra called over her shoulder, "Would you like to stay and have a bite with me?"

"Oh, I wouldn't want to impose, Sambra. I'm just supposed to drop this off."

Sambra lifted the tray out of the box, smelled under the lid of the tinfoil, and nodded her head. "Just as you said. Smells delicious." She pushed the tea towels and the box aside, ran around the countertop, and pulled down two plates. "I'm not taking no for an answer."

"Well, in that case, I'm stuck. You got me. For better or worse."

Sambra turned to her side and stared at Gina. "What an odd thing to say?"

"Sorry?"

"For better or for worse, in sickness and in health. They don't tell you about what you do after death, do they?"

Gina was all of a sudden extremely uncomfortable. She thought perhaps Sambra didn't know their news, so she forgave her for the misspeak. "I am so sorry for your loss, Sambra. I can't imagine going through that. And I just want you to know that I'm here if you ever need to talk to somebody."

Sambra made sounds as she dished up the casserole mixture on each of the plates. She added two apples that she had cut, brought the plates over to the dining room table, and offered Gina a chair at the head. "Please."

Gina sat down.

She waited until Sambra picked up her fork before she began eating. Sambra commented about how wonderful the casserole tasted. And Gina fully agreed.

"I was actually quite surprised to see you at the funeral, Gina. I'd heard about your little medical procedure, and I was just surprised. I guess I was a little touched too. I couldn't believe how strong you were. You have to tell me how you managed to do that. I was like a piece of jello. The only thing holding me together was that I was so fucking angry at everything around me. I think it was the drugs they gave me. I just couldn't believe you of all people would come to his funeral."

"Why wouldn't I?"

"Because of your loss. Haven't you ever wondered? It's almost like we are all tied together in some cosmic drama or game."

"What are you talking about, Sambra?" Gina was beginning to feel uncomfortable, regretting that she'd agreed to stay and eat with her. Something about this woman wasn't right.

Sambra laughed. "You mean Kyle didn't tell you how many times I called him and Christy? How many times I told him that I hated your husband?"

Gina was completely shocked. "I never heard any of that. I'm not so sure Armando even knows."

"Think about it, Gina. You have trouble, legitimate medical issues, your husband stays by to take care of you, and therefore there's a vacancy on the team. And my husband goes on his very first mission to take his place. We both experience a loss. And the only difference between us is you have somebody to grieve with and the love of my life is gone forever. I can't stop thinking about that. I couldn't stop thinking about that all during the funeral. I think about it every night. I try not to hate your husband, but I'd be lying if I said that I didn't. And I'm so sorry. Here you brought over this beautiful dinner, and I'm being a bitch."

Gina was sad for this woman. She could see that

Sambra was wallowing in the pits of despair, and even though Gina had herself felt like she was completely crumbling apart, this woman sitting in front of her had gone all the way around the bend. There was no mending taking place on her insides. Gina didn't know what to do to make her feel better. But she tried.

"I am grateful that I have my family unit, my son and my husband. I'm grateful that he hasn't come back injured, although I know the effects of war are huge on him and he carries that burden. You have no idea what it takes to look at a man for five, six, seven, eight years, and see the effects of war on him, see how it changes his mood each time when he comes back, especially from a difficult deployment. It's like a little piece of him dies every time. They try to hide it, but ultimately, I think it affects all of them. And because it affects all of them, it affects all of us too, the kids, the parents."

Sambra nodded and made designs with her fork in the casserole remains. "I guess because we were only married a little over a year, I don't have all that history. Maybe I should feel grateful for that."

Gina could see she was openly crying—not hiding it at all. She was afraid to touch the widow. Hopefully, her voice could be soothing enough to express how she felt.

"Sambra, time heals everything. Someday, something else will happen, and you'll realize that, all of a sudden, you don't feel that way anymore. Someone else will walk into your life, and it will be like the whole world has opened up for you again. I grew up in a very difficult and dysfunctional family, where I saw tragedy on a daily basis. I became a police officer because that's where I was comfortable. Now I can see why I was so well-suited for it. It doesn't make it easy, but I learned how to set it aside and deal with it, to help those who are in trouble, and me. I guess of all the things I've done since I've been married, that's the thing I miss the most. I am a mother, and I have lost three children before they were born. That's just a fact. But I've had a good life, a good family, a good husband. And a bright future."

Gina leaned forward and delicately placed her hand on Sambra's forearm resting on the table.

"And I see the same for you. I really do. Someday, you'll find love again."

CHAPTER 7

ARMANDO HELD ONTO his sleeping son after peeling him from the car seat. He was at the front door, unlocking it with one hand, his other wrapped around his three-year-old's tiny waist. Headlights flashed on his back, and he recognized Gina's car. He quickly slipped open the door, leaving it ajar, and tiptoed down the hall to take Artemis to his bedroom.

He laid him on the bed, removed his pants and shoes, but left his shirt and underwear on. He handed Artemis his favorite toy, a stuffed camel Armando had brought back from one of his trips overseas. He turned on the nightlight, which flashed blue and green images of animals all around the room as the shade revolved around the bulb. Tucking the covers up around his chin, Artemis turned to his side, hugged the camel, and was fast asleep before Armando could leave the room. He left the door ajar.

Gina looked tired as she walked through the front

door.

"How did it go?" Armando asked. He was prepared for anything, even some kind of a snarky remark, which seemed to be what he was getting these days.

"I was glad I did it, Armando. Sambra is very needy, but inside, I think she has a heart somewhere. But man, she's hurting. And the reason it was good for me to see her is—"

She stared up into his eyes. He held his breath as he stepped closer to her, carefully. Her beautiful face shone in the shadows of their small living room, her black hair shiny and mussed. Even tired, Gina was more beautiful to him every day, every hour they were together. He was not quite close enough to be able to touch her. He did not want to spook her or appear too needy, but Armando did need anything she might give him. He licked his lips and listened.

"I got to see how lucky I am, how much better we have it here. And she said something to me that really made an impression."

"What?" He waited with bated breath, watching her expression. He thought he saw softness there. His desire for her was beginning to ramp up faster than he could control, but he enjoyed and even relished the feeling.

She quickly looked down at her feet and then continued.

"She said the only difference between me and her was that I got to grieve with you, whereas she had to grieve all by herself."

Armando took one careful step closer. In his deep husky voice, he whispered, "I'm glad you went, Gina. I'm glad you went out there, out of our world, and did something nice for somebody else. I think it's healthy to do that. It means a lot to me too. It means you are getting better. You're recovering. It's a very important step."

He watched her expression carefully as his words fell on her. Her breathing hitched a bit. Was this attraction brewing? Could he dare to assume her desire for him was returning? He hoped against everything sacred that it was.

Her body wobbled a bit, perhaps just now reacting to his closeness to her. He even heard her heart beating and knew in his gut it wasn't just nerves. She missed him. She missed his arms around her waist and the way he treated her, the way he loved her. She'd missed that. Had the iceberg in her heart begun to melt? He could only hope.

He kept the safe space between them, but he wanted to take her in his arms, especially when she didn't step back or cut off the intimacy rapidly approaching between them.

"Armando, I felt, until this afternoon, that I didn't

deserve to heal. I'm now ashamed to admit that."

"Did she talk about Erik?" he asked.

"A little. They've only been married a little over a year, and I didn't realize that. Her whole world is upside down really. She doesn't have much family, and I don't know anything about them."

He knew more about Sambra's background than he'd revealed to Gina, as Erik had confided to Kyle. She was an orphan child brought to the U.S. by a military commander in the field with a group of some dozen other children who lost parents in the war-torn region. The commander had flown a mercy mission to extract the youngsters from certain death. Sambra had been just a toddler and was injured, so the extraction was deemed critical.

Putting that aside for a later conversation, Armando carefully took one more step closer, and this time he rested his hands on her upper arms. At first, she flinched. Then she softened, even leaning forward toward him. It thrilled him that just the touch of his hands on her created such a reaction. It encouraged him, adding to the bonfire growing in his belly.

Carefully, he moved his fingers up to her face and smoothed over her cheek, stroking her skin, softly and without saying a word. Then his forefinger traced the outline of her lower lip.

Gina stepped back slightly, looked up to him, and

removed his hand from her face. But she held onto it as she dropped their hands between them. The mood had suddenly changed. He would wait, wait for her to soften again as he worked to self-correct the questions he had lingering in his heart.

"You said you wanted talk tonight?" she finally asked. Her eyes held a flirtatious light, her head tilted to the side.

His warm expression back to her sparked that molten need deep inside her. He saw it now. It was unmistakable. His breathing matched hers, deep and ragged. He felt like he was pulling from her all kinds of raw emotions, some of them negative, purging her body with waves of love. He could see her desire eliminate her resistance. She was becoming putty in his hands.

"Thank you, Gina. Thanks for giving me the chance to express this, because I felt it was important to tell you what I came up with today. I gave some consideration to what you said at the counselor." He stopped as his hand came up to her cheek again. Then he let it fall to his side and stood six inches from her body, her heat infusing into him, the sound of her breathing and the faint rumble of her stomach sent warmth as his heart began to melt for her, thawing his own resistance as well.

As she leaned toward him, she asked, "And?"

Gina looked up into his face, and it seemed like the most natural thing in the world to slip his arms around her waist, leading her arms up to his shoulders and lacing her fingers behind his neck.

She didn't flinch as he stepped closer and pressed his chest against hers, leaned in, and whispered into her ear, "I've decided, Gina, that if you really want to go back to work, that's what you should do. You've sacrificed for us, and now it is my turn. I want you to do exactly what you feel is necessary. I don't want to be a roadblock anymore. I just want a chance to help bring our love back. And I'd do anything in the world for it."

He kissed the side of her forehead and tucked her head into the space below his chin. He was thrilled she did not stiffen. Her hands gently cupped the back of his neck, one forefinger rubbing across his collar bone and perhaps aiming for purchase beneath his shirt. He rubbed the back of her head, lacing and fingering, sifting through her hair.

"Armando—" Her needy voice called out as she pressed against him and encouraged his arms to squeeze her tightly.

But he stopped her with a kiss. And then he deepened that kiss. Then he positioned himself in the opposite direction, going in deeper, pressing her against him, rubbing down along her rear and then back up again. He needed her, he thought as their mouths explored and teased together. He'd missed this tender part of her that matched so perfectly with what he wanted to show her. He felt every breath, every little moan as he stroked her, explored with his fingers some of the until now forbidden territories of her body. She opened, accepting his loving touch. He was thrilled at the permission, at the level of need he was now reading from her body.

She broke away from the kiss, swooning, wiping the errant strands of hair from her forehead, almost appearing dizzy from his kisses. "I'm still confused, Armando. I don't feel like I'm totally myself yet."

Armando tipped her head back and stared into her eyes, whispering, "Not a problem. We'll go very slow, Gina." He brushed his lips across hers.

He'd unleashed the floodgates. Filled with the passion he could see in her eyes as well as in the racing of her heart, she said, "I want you to try to heal me. Please. Show me how you can heal me."

She collapsed into him, bracing herself against his body. He was so ready for her, so ready to rock her world and show her everything about how he loved this woman.

He chuckled, joyous at the thought of what he anticipated would be a miraculous night together in each other's arms. It lightened his soul when he picked her up and carried her to their bedroom. She moaned and writhed in his arms. His package was getting so fucking hard he thought perhaps he'd burst from his jeans.

Laying her down carefully, he removed her shoes, delicately holding her ankles and encircling them with his hands. He kissed her knees as his hand moved up her body to slip off her clothing, starting with her pants. And then all she had on was her panties.

She rose up, reaching for his shirt buttons. Her bent knees revealed the wetness between her legs. His fingers relished breaching the tiny elastic bands of her panties until he teased to stroke her sex, but worked around her opening as she moaned and spread her knees wider, pushing herself against his fingers.

"Oh God, please!" she whispered.

"You like that? Are you hungry for this, Gina? Do you have any idea how much I want to fuck you, sweetheart?" he whispered.

She threw her head back and giggled.

"Help me get you naked, Armando. I need your body pressed against mine, and I need it now."

"Yes, ma'am. Are you going to cuff me too?"

"If you don't behave, I'm going to tie you up to the bed and screw your brains out."

"Such wicked punishment so lovingly delivered. I have lots to share with you. I've been saving it for way, way too long, Gina."

He removed her shirt and bra, kissing her nipples, and then rose. While she moved on the bed, he disrobed but was slow and clumsy about it. He grinned.

"Are you fucking around with me?" she asked with a sexy expression of surprise.

"I haven't begun fucking around with you, my dear. But trust me, when we're done, you'll feel thoroughly fucked, and you will love it," he said as he climbed over her, using his shoulders under her knees to lift them and give himself full access to her throbbing and swollen sex.

He gently extracted her fingers from her opening and replaced them with his shaft, after removing the last barrier between them. The feel of her warm, moist flesh inside engorged him fuller. He thrust deep and slowly withdrew, only to thrust again.

"I've been a fool, Armando," she said as she squeezed his buttocks and accepted him fully.

"No, sweetheart, you were saving it up for this. This makes up for everything. I'd gladly go through the last few weeks again and again if this was always the outcome. I love you so much, sweetheart. I will never stop. I will never be able to help myself from loving you, no matter what you do."

Her hands framed his face. "Thank you. Thank you for loving me the way I didn't deserve."

"Nonsense, you shouldn't say that. You deserve it

all, Gina. We both do."

"I've missed you."

"Baby, I've been here all along. I'm not going anywhere. I want you to show me what's in your heart. Remind me that you'll never leave my side. I need to feel your love, Gina."

By the light of the early fall moon, Armando took his time and brought her back to life, kiss by kiss by kiss. Her tears soaked the pillow as he worshiped her body well into the early hours of the morning. It was something only he could do.

They were home at last.

CHAPTER 8

G INA GOT THE call from the San Diego Police
Department on the day Armando found out
Team 3 would be deploying to North Africa in two
weeks. She was apprehensive about starting a new job,
even though Armando had given his blessing. It was a
spot in the traffic division, which she readily accepted
before she heard about Armando's news.

She was going to be partnered with a veteran officer who had once worked narcotics, but he had been
demoted due to an officer-involved shooting and
disappearance of contraband and much needed
evidence that would have been helpful to build their
case against the drug lord. That part of her assignment,
she didn't care for.

Her captain told her she was being placed with the
disgraced officer so that she could keep an eye on him.
And the captain expected Gina to report the truth
about his behavior. She didn't like this man's future

with the force left solely in her hands. She also knew Armando wouldn't like the situation either. She almost took back the offer but decided to wait until after she'd talked to her husband.

"I don't want you to tell anyone," her captain began. "And I'd prefer it if you not tell your husband, either. But I understand you will have to do what you have to do, and I have no right to interfere with your marriage. I just want it made clear, if anything goes on that you're suspicious of or you see that there's any inkling of him being a dirty cop, I want to know about it right away. And I'm telling you now before you develop a friendship and a comradery, which is normal and even helpful in situations like this."

Gina agreed and told him she would be discussing it with Armando.

"If you weren't married to one of the Navy's finest, I would insist. But I trust him as I trust you, Gina. Don't let me down."

"I won't, sir."

When she got home and explained to Armando about the assignment, she was hoping he'd be more excited than he was. But then, when he told her about the due date of their deployment, she could see he was worried. He was also concerned about the choice of partner. He said so, yet left the decision up to her.

"I don't like you having to be a tattletale, especially

with a guy who's been dirty or been demoted for being possibly dirty. That's not the kind of person who's going to have your back."

Armando looked into her eyes, holding the tops of her shoulders while he did so.

"Gina, I'm all for this new gig for you, but let's be smart about it."

"I promised—I promised the captain that I would do what he's asked me. I think the captain will have my back if something should happen, and you and I both know what I think of dirty cops. I mean, I saw a lot of that in undercover work. Isn't that part of what we do?"

Armando stepped away and nodded, scratching his chin and staring at one of their child's toys on the carpet. "You do what you have to do, sweetheart. I said I would support you, and I will. I just want you to be smart. And I know you are, and I know you're dedicated, and they're lucky to have you. I'm proud of you."

"Just like Kyle's lucky to have you on Team 3. You guys are the good guys, the white hats, right? You're always telling me that anyway."

"Fair enough. You give it a shot. And then promise me we can have that discussion. When do you start?"

Gina fidgeted with her fingers and bit her lower lip. "He wants me to come in tomorrow to sign the paperwork. I accepted the job, but I didn't sign up. There's stuff they have to do to put things back in my pension, and I've opted to have them take as much out as I'm allowed, so we can be building that nest egg for Artemis. I want to make sure he gets to go to college, a chance you and I didn't get."

"I got you, Gina. We'll do that. And when's the first day, really official day on the job?"

"He said I could be riding patrol as soon as Wednesday. And when do you leave for Africa?"

"Two weeks from Wednesday."

She could see that his level of concern had risen. It was one thing to go off to deployment in a dangerous place, but it was another thing to have his wife operate with a less than stellar partner, and he wondered if he should try to intervene and talk to the captain himself. At least that's what he suggested to Gina.

"Don't you dare, Armando. I want to do this my way. I know you worry. You're going to have to trust me. I trust you."

"But I've got two hundred guys on SEAL Team 3 and the platoon that we travel with as backup. Any one of those guys would die for me, Gina. That's not what you've got here. You're headed off into San Diego proper, making stops, and who knows who you're going to get? Who knows if some felon with a trunk full of guns forgot to get his license renewed or was driving around on stolen plates? You know that happens. We read about it every day."

"I get it. I'm going to wear your Kevlar vest that you got for me, not the police issue, and I promise to take all the precautions."

"And you do the searches in the car. You let your partner go confront the guy, the driver. You make him be the first line of contact, sweetie. Besides, he's senior. That's how it's done."

"I will if I can. And that's a promise. I will be careful, Armando. Please trust me."

THE NEXT MORNING, Gina made it to the station meeting and then with her former union rep and the personnel secretary. She signed the department's paperwork, agreed to a medical physical, and had the blood draw, which was a new protocol now.

"Bloodwork? Already?" she asked as the technician left.

"Requirement of all new hires. Federal mandate. We've been slapped with some extra things coming down from Washington."

Gina knew what all this was for. They were just making sure that she didn't have substance abuse issues or other medical reasons for not being employable.

"So that should do you, Gina," Shirley, the HR secretary, said to her. She stood and extended her hand across the desk. "Welcome to the force. I hope it's a long and fruitful career, Gina. And we're rooting for you. We need more women in the department. This will also help our ratios, big time. You were a valuable asset to this department when you worked undercover, but now it's even more important than before. So thank you for stepping up to the plate."

Gina stood and shook her hand.

Garner Townsend, Gina's new partner, was a formidable character. His voice was loud, and Gina had heard him make jokes and comments in the squad room on earlier occasions. She noted that he didn't appear to be well-liked. He was best known for being a ladies' man, divorced, but he reminded everyone he'd also been married four times.

"Most people don't give me credit for marrying the women I date. You're not going to hold that against me are you, Gina?" he asked her when they got in the patrol car.

"Well, I let you drive, so I guess that's endorsement enough. I understand you're single now, but are you working on number five?" Gina asked him.

"Absolutely not. I'm done with women for the time being. Besides, little lady..." He was going to place his hand on her right shoulder and thought better of it.

"Good idea, Garner. I don't want you to touch me unless you ask permission. Every single time," Gina said.

"You got it," he answered with a shrug as he started the car, and they headed through the lot onto the street.

The day was going to be a nice one. As fall days turned into winter, the San Diego area would often have a hot snap before it started to get colder. Rain was still pretty non-existent, but the hot dry heat was always something Gina didn't care for. She would've taken the rain anytime.

During the day, she noted her partner seemed to be well put together. His demeanor on traffic stops, writing tickets, and responding to minor traffic accidents was pretty straightforward, and his social skills were excellent. He comforted elderly people who were injured in accidents, he was great with kids and women, and he had a healthy respect for the general public as a whole. He didn't care for sheriff's deputies or other departments in law enforcement, and he also disliked some of the military police. He told Gina he felt they threw their weight around too much and tried to get his "nickers twisted"—with finger quotes.

"Nickers twisted?" Gina asked, her nose wrinkling up.

"My mother used to read those books, you know the ones with the guys that were naked on the cover?"

"Oh, you mean romance books? Is that what you

mean?"

"Smut books. She was a nice lady, but she liked smut books."

"Well, I like romance novels. And for your information, they're not all smut books. Some of them don't have any sex in them at all. Although, I seem to like the ones that do." She glared at him because he was going to blurt out something she knew she wasn't going to want to hear. She pressed her hand to within inches of his face. "Let me stop you right there and tell you I don't like necessarily reading the sex books. I just like to have some kind of heat between the hero and the heroine. I want to see how they meet, fall in love, and how they get it on."

"Should I tell the captain about this?" he asked her. He was chuckling to himself.

"Don't put anything into this, or I will sue your ass," Gina said. And then she started to laugh as well. "I don't ask you at all about your dates, and I'm never going to. And I have no interest in talking to you about your former wives, your girlfriends, your former girlfriends, or anybody you date now. I have no interest in it. But if somebody gives me a nice romance book where the hero and heroine get together in the end and they have that happily ever after, I'm all for it. We don't have enough of that, do we?"

He shook his head as they left a convenience store

parking lot. "I guess you're right. I stand corrected."

Gina was about to say something when a car appeared from nowhere and slammed broadside into the patrol car. Unfortunately, it was on Gina's side.

The last she heard was a loud crash, a boom, and a huge flash of light.

CHAPTER 9

A RMANDO WAS AT the duck club gun range instructing four new additions to SEAL Team 3. The range had a public facility with memberships sold to the general public. But in the rear, there was a gun range housed in bunkers dug into the side of a hill, with long lanes constructed with concrete blocks. This was where special units were allowed to train, including the SEALs. But occasionally police and ATF task forces used the facility too.

Armando was giving them information about what kinds of weapons they would need to bring on their next deployment and how to carry their ammo. By practicing shooting with each one of them, he carefully made sure they knew how to sight their weapons. He showed them some of his firepower and choices they could make, if they so decided. He also explained about the terrain and how to compensate for the hot wind, sometimes navigating the smoke and wildfires and some of the situations they might find themselves in the middle of from his previous trips to Africa.

"It's not one of my favorite places, gents. A lot of stuff going on. It's hard for a small cadre—even though we're well trained—to come up against some of these larger militias. And a lot of the times, our State Department has had negotiations with the government proper, but the land often is ruled by the warlords. Learning who is your enemy and who is your friend is a very big part of what you'll be doing over there. The quicker you learn that and to read people as far as who you can trust, the longer you'll survive. And you may save someone like me, like your LPO, like anyone else on the team, from a tragedy."

He picked up his M4 and was about to demonstrate something when one of his guys nodded in the direction behind him. He turned around.

Armando's heart sank as he saw Kyle and Cooper running full tilt toward him. He could tell from the expression on Kyle's face that he wasn't going to like the news. He carefully set his M4 on the table in front of him. He braced for the words that were coming his way.

Out of breath, Kyle pulled him aside, and with Cooper, they both put their hands on each of his shoulders. Kyle was the first to speak. Armando didn't take his eyes off of his LPO.

"It's Gina. She's been involved in an accident. And I just wanted to come get you and make sure that you heard it from me. I think you better gather your gear and come with us."

Cooper turned around and addressed the men Armando had been working with. He began stashing Armando's duty bag with equipment and things that he had brought with their input.

Armando's shocked silence was all he could give. "Is she…?"

"She's alive, but we know she's badly hurt. It was not a police-related incident, although she was in the squad car. Someone hit her."

"So where is she at?"

"They airlifted her to Scripps. Armando, they had to cut her out of the car."

"Geez!" His insides were like ice.

"If necessary, they may be taking her elsewhere. But as you know, they are a Level 1 trauma center, so she's in good hands, Armando. And we know for a fact she's alive."

"Okay, I got to get over there. I want to make sure—"

"TJ is over there right now and he's going to make damn sure that the medical staff is up to speed, and they are doing everything they should be to make sure she survives. Does she have any medical conditions that you know about?"

Armando could feel the hot tears in his eyes as he grabbed the duty bag Cooper had over his shoulder and started running for his car. "Other than the fact she lost a baby a month ago, I think everything is okay with her. That's something I think she's recovered from." He wiped the tears defiantly from his eyes with the tips of his fingers as he ran, giving Kyle a scowl.

His hands shaking, Armando fished for his keys until Cooper grabbed them.

"Armani, you're in no shape to drive. And I know for a fact Kyle is a hell of a faster driver than you are. So I'm going to take your truck over to the hospital so you'll have it. But you ride with Kyle. And I'm insisting."

"I got it."

He sat next to Kyle as his LPO roared through the gates of the gun range. His heart was melting, the pit in his stomach told him this was all wrong. He'd known he didn't want her to go back to work, and this, her very first day back on the job, this is what she got?

Kyle whispered as he drove. "You know, Armani, we got to keep ourselves level-headed here. Don't go putting yourself through purgatory thinking about what could happen. You want to just stay level. We'll find out in due time what we have to do. And we'll do what we do, right?" Kyle turned and looked at him.

Armando couldn't return his gaze. "It's just been such a roller coaster, Kyle. If something's happened—"

"Now that's what I'm talking about, Armani. You don't go doing that, you hear? You keep it level. You keep it between the lines. If we got to yell and scream and shout at somebody, we will. And we'll do it together."

That didn't really satisfy him, but he had no choice. Kyle wasn't going to let him get out of control with his emotions. And he agreed it was good they hadn't let him drive.

Of all the things he thought he would encounter this year or in the years to come, this was the one event he never thought he would. This was the one thing that he didn't prepare for. And now he wished he had.

"I better call my mom. I'm sure she'll keep Artemis an extra night or two, or whatever."

"You do that. And if you need backup to that, Christy would be happy to. Don't worry. The Team will get that duty covered. You just be with Gina."

Armando discovered that Felicia had already been called. Someone from the force had given Mayfield a heads-up. She was beside herself wanting to rush to the hospital, but she hadn't wanted to miss Armando's call or abandon Artemis.

"What is her condition? Please, Armando, tell me she is still fighting. Is she badly injured?"

"I'm not sure. But I need you to stay there with Artemis. I need you to be his leveling influence. I'll handle telling him about his mom when we know. Thank you so much, Mom, and please let Mia know too. Maybe she can bring some of her brood over and you guys can watch all the kids together."

"That's a good idea, son. That would be good for your little angel. You just go be with your wife. And please let me know."

It took forever to arrive at the Emergency Center due to the late afternoon traffic. Kyle pulled up to the rear ER lobby, and before he stopped the car, Armando had opened the door and was running inside. The reception area was packed with people filling just about every chair. He spoke to the security officer manning the desk.

"I'm Armando Guzman. My wife, Gina, was brought in here. She's a cop. An auto accident, I understand. Where is she, please? I need to see her."

The policeman asked one of the admitting nurses to come get him and take him to the back. They brought him into one of the treatment rooms, pulling the curtain aside and asking him to take a seat on the bed.

Armando protested. "I need to see her. I must see her."

"And you will. One of your teammates is with her

now. I'm going to bring him over. I believe she's in surgery, sir. I don't want to interfere with what the doctors are doing."

The nurse, although very stern, gave a hopeful smile to him. He hoped against hope that Gina was going to survive or that her wounds were not going to be life-changing.

Just before the nurse left, Armando asked if there was another driver involved.

"I'm not at liberty to discuss this. We are still notifying his next of kin. I'm sure you understand patient confidentiality. Just wait here for your teammate.

Seconds later, TJ pulled back the screen, swearing, and grabbed Armando by the arm. "I'm going to take you down the hallway toward the OR. You don't say anything, Armani. You act like you're supposed to be here. And don't look like a worried husband. I'm going to try to get you in to see her. But I'm not sure I can."

"How bad is it, TJ?" Armando said as he ran to keep up with his tall team medic.

"I'm not going to lie to you, Armani. It's bad. It's very bad."

Armando closed his eyes, clenched his right hand into to a fist, and stopped. He didn't want to ask, but he had to. "Is she still alive?"

TJ yanked on his arm again, pulling him down the hallway and through a double set of windowed doors, which flapped behind them violently. Without looking at Armando, TJ said, "I'm not sure."

Armando was furious with the whole world for just a split second. He was furious with God for having rained down such horrible news. Just when their life was getting back together, just when all things suddenly seemed to be possible again, now this. He said a prayer, but he didn't feel anybody was upstairs to hear him. And that pissed him off even more.

Two doctors stood in the hallway. One was still masked up, the front of his green scrubs covered with blood. The other one had removed his mask and was nodding his head to some of the information he was being told. They both turned in Armando's direction. He didn't recognize either one of them. But they looked at TJ and then back at Armando, and he understood they knew TJ was a SEAL Team 3 medic. In unison, both doctors shook their heads very slowly and examined the floor.

Armando flew into a rage, grabbing one of the surgeons. "No! No, this cannot be." He looked at TJ. "Do something. You go see her. Can you do anything, TJ?"

TJ shook his head. "These are the best that we have. I'm going to let them explain it to you. And I'm going to sit right here next to you while you listen. She's out of pain now, Armando. Focus on that. She's not going to feel any more pain or trauma. She's gone, Armando, and I know you have a strong faith. I know you believe in Heaven." TJ held Armando's face between his strong hands. "You've got to hang onto that and know she's in a better place. It's just not here, with you."

Armando had been searching for words that TJ wouldn't give him, couldn't give him. His insides had frozen. He was going to throw up. Nothing in his chest cavity was working. He gulped in air as TJ gently felt his pulse and held him tight, until Armando began to sob. And then he grabbed the back of TJ's shirt, digging his fingernails through the fabric to his flesh underneath. He knew he was going to cause a welt, but he desperately needed somebody to hang onto.

CHAPTER 10

THEY LAID GINA'S body on a covered gurney. She'd been covered with a fresh white sheet, but red blotchy marks had already soaked through areas in the middle of her chest. Though they tried to clean her up, blood and tissue lodged in the strands of her beautiful, shiny black hair.

He'd seen men die in combat, men still alive with arms and legs strewn all over the battlefield somewhere. He'd seen men who were dead that didn't realize they were dead yet. He'd seen so many unspeakable horrors, including the civilians, especially the children and women, who had been tortured, killed, or just plain caught in the wrong place at the wrong time. He was prepared for that. Except he could never have prepared to see Gina's lifeless body on the gurney. In front of him.

Kyle was on one side of the gurney, and TJ stood beside him on the other. Kyle was the first to speak up.

"Armani, do you want to be alone? Just let me know."

Armando's stiff hand and fingers reached for the sheet that covered Gina's face. He didn't answer Kyle, but he pulled back the covering and wept when he saw her beautiful skin, marred with multiple flecks from probably an exploding window or objects inside the car. She didn't look dead, because her color was still good. He wanted to hold her hand, but he couldn't find it. TJ stopped him and shook his head.

"Where is her arm, her right arm?"

"Armani, it's best if you just don't look. I don't think it's here." TJ himself was crying, tears streaking down his cheeks. He put his hand around Armando's back, his fingers up over his shoulder, and then he tapped him gently. Whispering carefully, he said, "You got this, man. We're all right here with you. You got this."

Armando used his forefinger to trace the outline of her lips, which were still supple, although they had begun to turn purple. He breathed deeply, as he knew he should, just to keep his wits about him. He didn't want to pass out like someone who didn't know better. He was stronger than this. Somehow, he would live again. And remembering Artemis, somehow he was going to be able to explain this to his son.

One of the two surgeons came inside and took the

sheet from Armando's hand, placing it back over her face. He looked up at him. "What is it you need to know?"

"How—how did this happen? What happened to her?"

"From what someone on scene told the paramedics, somebody T-boned their cruiser. The other car was traveling at a tremendous rate of speed. We think in excess of 60 miles an hour, and they flew, literally flew into the cruiser. The driver of the vehicle had three others in the car with him, and they all perished. The impact turned their Cadillac into a suitcase."

"They had no chance, Armando," said TJ. "None of them had a chance."

"But she lived after the impact?"

"She never gained consciousness, Armando. Technically, she might have been alive, but these were not survivable wounds. She was pretty torn up. I don't think she felt a thing. I know she didn't suffer long."

The doctor motioned for them to leave the room. Armando couldn't do anything but obey.

ARMANDO ASKED THE police who arrived at the scene if there were any survivors. He was told absolutely not. Gina's partner hadn't died from a heart attack, as someone had mentioned. He died because he literally had been crushed to death by the steering wheel and the motor based on the angle of the impact. Gina had airbags on both sides, and that protected her somewhat, but it wasn't enough to save her life. The officer gave his condolences. The second officer responding was in tears himself, a young cadet right out of school. Right out of the academy, he said.

The next thing Armando heard was the sound of his mother's voice screaming as she ran down the hallway toward him.

"No, no, no! This cannot be, my son. Please tell me they have made a mistake here. I cannot bear this. I just cannot bear this." She buried her head in Armando's chest. He looked up at his stepfather, a retired police officer himself, and both men shared their extensive anguish and pain at the horrors and sights they had both seen during their careers. Gus whispered something that Armando couldn't hear. And then his mother was sobbing so uncontrollably that Mayfield took her in his arms and started to lead her outside.

Armando thought that was best. Kyle was still there, and he whispered, "We've got Artemis over at the Lansdowne household. He's having a good time, and I have it on good authority he is eating ice cream with whipped cream on it.

Armando was grateful. Thank God for the little joys of life. He wasn't sure there were enough of them, however. But he'd try to look for them, just the same.

Even though it might be an exercise in futility.

The next two days went by in a blur. Armando spent most of his time drinking whiskey and eating only what he was forced to eat. Food began piling up, because the food chain was working overtime. Several of his buddies took turns babysitting him, and there was no time at all that he was left alone. Kyle had all of his guns and ammo removed from his house. And he even had Dr. Brownlee, Cooper's father-in-law and a well-known psychiatrist, stop by for a home visit. Armando accepted all of this, although his anger was building, and he was about ready to send everyone home.

"I'm not an invalid. And I'm not going to knock my head off." He had said that so many times to various people in his house, he was getting tired of repeating himself.

Christy and several of the wives helped him with the funeral arrangements. They carefully and lovingly handled all the details after discussing it with him. A get-together was planned at the house after the funeral. They told him if he wanted to just stay in the bedroom and not come out and talk to everyone, that it would be his choice. But they encouraged him to stay connected to the group and let the group heal him.

As the next few days passed, Kyle and the team began to get ready for the deployment. Armando drove himself over to the team building and shocked the group when he walked in, sitting in the back row. The metal chair beneath him squeaked. There were some whispers, but most everybody accepted his desire to stay involved in the mission.

After the meeting, he met with Kyle.

"I'm not sure I can let you go, Armani. I think I got to get a sign off from Dr. Brownlee or somebody. I just wouldn't feel right."

"You've got to let me go, Kyle. I need this. I need to be trusted, and I need to show that I can do this."

"If you were injured in an accident or a mission of some kind, there are rules about that, Armani. In this case, I don't know what the Navy says about it or if they have the right to exclude you, but trust me, if the brass thinks you're not ready, you're not going. And I'm not going to stake my career defending you, under the risk of sending you to your own grave. You want to kill yourself, you don't do it under the Navy's command or under my command. You take care of that when you come home. Or while you're home. You understand this, Armando?"

"I do."

"So if they tell me you can't go, it's a no-go. It's just a fucking no-go. And I don't think it's a very bright idea to do this."

Armando could see Kyle was livid about even being

placed in this position to tell him he couldn't join the rest of the team. But he was absolutely right. If the LPO made a mistake on this one, it could be career ending. Armando didn't wish that on Kyle.

"I think I can do it. And I think, if I don't do it, it's just going to prolong all this shit that's going on inside me. I will take whatever consequences come my way, and if you think I'm not up to speed or up to my duties, anything you see, you can yank me out and send me home. I give you full autonomy to do so."

"You forget, Armani, that may not be convenient for us to do. You know as well as I do what some of that terrain looks like. Some of those places aren't even passable this time of year. You'd have to be Tarzan himself to make it out on your own. And I can't risk guys I don't have to take you out. So you just better fucking step up to the plate. And I'll scream at you and yell at your ass, and I'll keep you tied up in a tent before I'll let you go out and do something crazy. This is going to be a really tough mission. And I don't want you causing somebody else some kind of distraction that's going to end in injury. That's the bottom line. I'm looking out for everybody, not just you. So you might want to consider, sailor, that this is a selfish request on your part. And I don't like it one bit."

"Just try. Please try."

Armando met again with Dr. Brownlee in his office

in downtown San Diego. It had been years since he'd met the man professionally. After the death of Mrs. Brownlee, he had pulled back on his office hours and gone into semi-retirement. The doctor also had become acquainted with a woman from his deceased brother's past. He found out many years later that she had born him a child, a daughter, and he was getting used to his new family. It was like having a part of his brother, Will, back again.

"But enough about me. How are things really going, Armando? Are you going to make me a liar if I recommend you're cleared to go."

"I don't wish that on anyone. But, sir, I think I'm good."

"Hell you are. No way you are, Armando. But can you function one hundred percent?"

"I'm working at one hundred twenty, I think, sir."

"How are you sleeping?" Brownlee's lean frame was dressed in casual golf clothes. Armando figured his morning had been consumed with one of his passions, which was golf.

"I'm sleeping okay. I spent the first week, as you probably know, getting drunk almost every night. But I am back to be being full-time dad now, and Artemis and I are a joy to each other. I don't want to lie and tell you I don't miss her, but the nightmares, the sweats, and the binges of alcohol, they're pretty much done,

Dr. Brownlee."

"How are you thinking? I mean, are you able to rationalize things, figure things out? Have you tried playing any card games, resumed your workout routine?"

"I've never been one for board games or card games. I'm sorry. I'm a man of action. I don't like to gamble, and I hate playing cards."

"Probably a good idea. I know I'd have a little more money in my retirement if I didn't like to go to the casino now and then. But that's a whole other story."

Armando chuckled. He needed to ask Dr. Brownlee a question, and he was hesitant to form the words.

"Go right ahead. I'll let you know if it's something I can't reveal. But ask me whatever you want. This is your time."

"Kyle and Cooper said that you've started a new relationship? I was just wondering how that happened, and how you felt about it. How long did it take before you could even feel somewhat normal?"

"Well, usually I wouldn't talk about it, but you guys are like family to me, and Libby is married into the Brotherhood. I'd be not at my full capacity if I didn't give you what my personal experience has been. Carla and I were so happily married for all those nearly forty years, I was not prepared for her passing, and in the scheme of things, it happened very quickly. But you know how fate is, right?"

"Exactly. I know how fate is."

"Before she passed, we got a visit from my niece, a niece I never knew I had, and the spitting image of her dad, Will, which means she looks like a daughter I could have. She offered to bring her mother by. I wasn't going to meet her unless Carla said it was okay. I just didn't think it was fair to Carla. She seemed to be fine, although I will tell you she watched me every chance she could get." Dr. Brownlee stared down at Armando over the tops of his glasses. "I mean, that woman could get secrets out of a deaf turnip."

Armando laughed at his lack of vocabulary skills. "A deaf turnip, huh?"

"I don't know what you call it. But she could literally get anything out of anybody. You guys should have used her in some of your snatch and grabs. That woman was deadly. Even if I had any thoughts of straying, you know, to the side, there's no way I would've gotten away with it. Carla would've nailed my butt right away. And that's the way I liked it, to be honest. But boy, did she have her eagle eye on me. At the very end, she seemed to encourage our friendship. And I'd have to say that we are more friends than we are anything else. We're not married, and we're not living together, but we are good friends. And that started years and years ago with Will. That's always remained. Although she's very different than Carla, she and I are learning how little we have in common." Dr. Brownlee gave Armando a sly smile.

"So you're kind of having fun then?"

Dr. Brownlee's eyes flashed with a twinkle. "I'd have to say I am. I really am. She's a delightful lady, and she pushes me along. I don't know, I guess she makes me feel younger. She's a great companion, and she loves to travel. I look forward to someday being able to do more of that. Carla was always so sick that we couldn't do those trips that we had always talked about."

Armando could see that Dr. Brownlee's demeanor had changed and gone darker.

The doctor forced a small smile. "I'm sorry about that. I probably shouldn't have said anything. But I will tell you that I have not yet counseled a single person who ever thought they did everything they wanted to do with their spouse before their spouse passed. It's a universal problem for all humans. It was the same for me. I'm sure you're thinking of all the things that you and Gina weren't able to do, the things she can't do with Artemis. I'm just here to tell you that's normal. Put it behind you, and move forward."

CHAPTER 11

S AMBRA GUNNERSON WAS done with her grieving, or so she thought. She hadn't quite forgiven the military, specifically the Navy and more even Armando, for the death of her husband. But she knew logically they were not the ones at fault. She just couldn't bring herself to forgive. That was going to take another huge step in a direction she wasn't ready for. She saw it as a sign of weakness. Her nature was to fight, to show her fists and teeth and get even, not soften her heart.

While she heard the news of Gina Guzman's death, she was sad for their little boy and sad for Gina, who she could have become friends with, given time, but she did not feel sorry for Armando. In some cosmic way, God unleashed on him the exact same thing she was dealing with. And she felt he deserved it. It was part of her revenge, that black slimy pit deep inside her stomach.

She decided she'd consider moving out of state, perhaps up to the Pacific Northwest or some other place where she was an unknown, after her Navy lease expired. But she had nine months to stay, rent-free, and all of the medical bills and Navy-related expenses and insurance would continue. They hadn't had enough time to save much money, so she needed to rely on his death benefit and the insurance to make ends meet. She bitterly admitted to herself it kept her from having to take a job she'd hate, like a barista or something.

But she knew now was the time to start looking for a job, so she could begin the detachment from the military and its claws. She looked for something outside the San Diego area, something north, closer to LA, somewhere she could drive to but still live near the base where their rental was.

Reviewing the classifieds was an endless and boring job. It was useless checking out things for which she had no training. She didn't have a college degree. Erik was her whole life, and they had married young, so at twenty-one years of age, she didn't have much work experience either.

Erik's parents were good at sending her little things, like gift cards and hand-made crafts Erik's mother made to make her feel loved. Her hand-knitted comforters and embroidered pillowcases came nearly every month. She understood it was done to keep a mother's memory of her son alive. It wasn't really about helping his widow to heal.

The numbness in her life made it impossible to really enjoy those things, no matter how heart-felt they were intended.

Sambra's parents had faded into the mountains of Colorado, lost in their family business of running a restaurant and local ice cream parlor all the kids in high school hung out at as she was growing up. Even though outward appearances might dictate otherwise, she wasn't ever very close to them, although she tried to be cordial. After Erik's death, they made it clear they hoped she'd find another military man to help support her. Never being a very affectionate family, Sambra felt the sight of her made them afraid, since they were not equipped to help her deal with her loss.

So Sambra was all alone. Completely alone. Even though the casseroles kept coming and the home visits, although less and less frequent, were still happening.

Erik's parents attended the funeral; hers did not. And she could count on one hand the number of times she'd spoken to them since her husband's death.

Her skin was thickening. Her shoulders were broad enough to handle anything else that life could toss her way, as if she didn't have a right to be happy or have an easy life at all. It had started out that way, and perhaps it was destined, no matter what country she was raised in, no matter which set of parents she inherited.

It was what it was.

And it sucked.

Today she sat at her favorite coffee shop and scanned The Shopper magazine, that rag that was filled with more personals than news or legitimate advertising. But in the back, they had a series of columns for help wanted and services needed. She scanned the page.

Something popped out at her, and she immediately looked closer, reading the small print.

Were you adopted as a refugee child from Iran, Syria, or Iraq? Are you curious about your family left behind? Confidential immigration attorney seeks adoptees brought to the US at a young age. I can put you back in touch with your family roots.

His name was Assad Nefrusia. He had an office in downtown Los Angeles on Wilshire Boulevard.

Sambra dialed the number, and after the recording, she left a message.

It only took twenty-four hours for the attorney to call her back.

"So you are from Iran, Syria, or Iraq, is that correct?" the attorney's voice was husky like a heavy smoker and had a thick Middle Eastern accent.

"Yes, from Syria."

"And do you remember your parents?" he asked.

"No, I believe I was just a baby. I don't have any recollection of Syria or living in an orphanage there or anything. All my memories are of being here in the United States with my parents—with my adoptive parents, that is."

"Were you abused?"

"No, not at all. That's not why I'm calling. They were good people."

"So what has brought you to want to research your family lineage?"

"I saw a television program recently about refugee children being purchased and sold overseas. I'm sure my parents weren't involved in anything like that, but they had no children of their own, and I think they were just lonely people who wanted a child. I'm not so sure that the organization they hired was reputable, however. I seem to recall my mother said they were a little bit shady. But I honestly don't remember. I was about five or six then."

"Okay. But I have to ask you, are your parents still alive because I'm not understanding why now you wish to reconnect? Will they take kindly to you reaching out to your birth family of origin?"

"Because I've just lost my husband. We were married for about a year, year-and-a-half. I met him while he was training to become a Navy SEAL. He became a Navy SEAL, and he was killed on his very first deployment. I feel like I barely knew him, and I don't know much about his family, and I don't feel close to them. I was wondering if now might be a good time just to see if I have relatives. Perhaps I have family here in the States that I'm not even aware of. I just sort of feel like I'm in limbo. I'm living on his death benefit, so I can't spend a lot of money. I'm just curious more than ever. And I need something to do with my life."

"I completely understand, Sambra." The attorney was tapping something like a pencil or a pen on his desk. She could hear the ricochet in the background. And then the squeak of his office chair, and then his sigh before he answered her.

"I think I can help you. What sometimes has happened is that these adoptions that take in place are done for profit and the records are not available. Children get adopted who are not really orphans, and they are raised without knowing anything about the family who lost them. Of course, in many cases they've given up their children so that they have a chance at a better life elsewhere, so they may think they're rescuing their child. I'm not necessarily opposed to that, but sometimes, they are taken away from families who would be able to take care of them. And I don't know that about your case, but I can certainly find out."

He asked her about the circumstances of the military commander who facilitated her adoption. He also asked her if she knew what village or town she was from, which she didn't, and after taking down answers to all those questions, he promised to try his best to find her answers.

"I have contacts all over the Middle East. With all the wars and the families moving back and forth, the huge refugee issues going on all over Europe and the United States, the innocent children, the babies are sometimes just left out of the equation. My job is to help connect people with those of their kind."

"Their kind?" Sambra wasn't sure that she liked the tone of his voice, but she understood what he was trying to do.

"Someone from their culture, their birthright, Sambra. That was stolen from you, even though it saved your life, probably."

"I see. And how long will this take, this research?" she asked.

"I will call you next week sometime. And, my dear, thank you for calling."

SAMBRA APPLIED AT various temp agencies and then decided to go into Los Angeles proper to see if Amazon or one of the large retail outlets were hiring unskilled workers. She was smart, she knew English, and she could read. She just had no formal education, after dropping out in the eleventh grade and never getting her high school diploma. She had moved near the beach in San Diego and met Erik, and that changed her trajectory forever.

She asked to be taken off the widows' list, because she informed Christy and several of the other women that she wasn't really interested in staying involved in the SEAL community. Christy tried to talk her out of it, but she insisted.

"I have to do this my way. This was Erik's life. It wasn't really mine. Not yet. This is what he wanted. I need to find out what I want."

Christy still suggested she avail herself of all the extra benefits she could while she remained in the housing that allowed for Naval assistance. "Please get some help, some counseling. And I can recommend some very good people if you like. In fact, I happen to know there's a very powerful women's group—all ages. Some are mothers, some are wives, but they've all lost someone. If you connect with a group like that, it might help you learn how to navigate faster or help give you clarity of what you want to do with the rest of your life. You're so young. But you have a lot of wonderful days ahead of you."

Sambra recalled the nice message that Gina had left

her just before she died.

"I'll give it a shot," she promised Christy.

True to his word, the attorney set an appointment for her to come into the office the following week.

"I have some news, not exactly perfect news, but it's a start. And just in case you are concerned, I'm going to do this particular search for you gratis. I'm not going to charge you. But I'd like you to reach out to others who are perhaps in the same position. Do you know other people like yourself who are foreign born but married and living a life in the United States that they would not have normally done?"

"I have met some, yes. I have a friend from Turkey who was adopted by a Jewish family, in Oxnard. She and I became friends at the library."

"Well, if she's interested in finding her roots, I'm not so sure about my sources in Turkey, but I am certainly willing to give it a try. So until next week then, you take care of yourself."

THE ATTORNEY'S OFFICE was on the backside of an open-air restaurant serving Middle Eastern food using a trailer kitchen, surrounded by apartments. Red neon Arabic letters were scrawled on the kitchen windows. The neighborhood was a bit neglected. Some of the windows on several surrounding buildings were boarded up. Gang tags were everywhere. She entered through the metal doorway and found a sparsely furnished office that was clean but completely devoid of anything personal on the walls or furniture.

He stood up and greeted her at the door, motioning for her to take a seat in front of his scratched and overly-cluttered wooden desk. She couldn't help but smell the cooking oils and strange aromas coming from the kitchen below.

"Does this make you hungry sitting here all day smelling all these foods? Is this part of your business as well?"

"What business?"

"The restaurant," she pointed out the window at the floor below.

He leaned back in his chair and laughed heartily. "No, my dear. They are friends of friends. But absolutely not. And to be honest with you, I prefer American food. But they are frequented by a large Middle Eastern population here. As you know, we have many from Iran living in Southern California, starting years ago with the Shah and his family. From Syria not quite so much, but Iran certainly. It's a gathering place. And I rather feel safe here."

"Do you speak Arabic?" she asked.

"Of course. I would not be able to speak to anyone without that skill. And you, do you speak other languages? Arabic perhaps?"

"No, I'm sorry." She searched his desk, her eyes lighting on the papers scattered in semi-organized piles. Several pictures appeared here and there, some of them appearing very old, and some quite recent.

"So what have you found?"

"I've discovered that you come from the village of Sarna. You were adopted in Fayetteville, North Carolina on January 23, 1999, and the non-profit or NGO group handling the adoption was East-West Agency from Colorado. I am not familiar with them, but you were sponsored by them when you came."

"I didn't know this. I thought someone from the military brought me over."

"Yes, and apparently their application to adopt you was denied, so you were placed into foster care with this agency."

"Was everything done legit, then?" she asked.

"I think as an organization, they probably are fine. One of the better ones. But there are some irregularities about your adoption that I'm concerned about."

"Such as?"

"I see from the papers that your adoption was sealed and then unsealed. And I'm not quite sure about why that occurred. Did your parents ever say anything about this?"

"No. They never did."

"You might want to ask them, but from the looks of

the paperwork, it appears you may have siblings. And you may have siblings that live in the United States."

"Really?" Sambra was excited to hear this news. "You mean real brothers and sisters of mine?"

The attorney leaned back in his chair, placing his hands behind his head. As his elbows outstretched Sambra saw huge sweat marks running down underneath his armpits.

"I don't know how many brothers and sisters you may have had or if they are still alive, but I feel fairly sure that you have at least one and maybe two brothers."

"And how do you know this?"

"My dear, Allah works in mysterious ways. Sometimes it's a case where someone wishes to reach out and someone else has decided it's also time to reach out. They occasionally meet in the middle. Sometimes it's a case where records get moved, shuffled to another department, and things are revealed that were withheld for years and years. An investigation may be launched by some congressional committee or action group. We never know where all this information comes from, and we have to leave no stone unturned. But without revealing my trade secrets," he placed his hand against his heart and bowed slightly, "I wish to tell you that I am fairly sure I have located one of your brothers and possibly two. And I won't know for a few more days, as

I'd like to see if there is a match. I need to speak to him first."

"But where does he live?"

"Right now, my dear, he does not live in the United States. But my understanding is he's coming back here. He once lived in the San Francisco area. Are you happy with this news?"

Sambra wasn't sure. The one door had closed on her American life. Was she ready to embrace another? Was she ready to embrace another culture, a new family member? She answered the attorney in the only way she felt possible.

"I'm delighted."

CHAPTER 12

THE MISSION WAS to verify the site of a UN genocide event. They were to go deep into the interior of Benin in Western Africa, near the Horn. That in and of itself wouldn't have been too difficult for the twelve-man squad Kyle had selected. They were running heavy on shooters and medics, because it was anticipated the trip would be extremely dangerous and the possibility of casualties very high. Men were asked to volunteer, and in most cases, the married men with young children chose or were encouraged not to go. But Armando knew he had to be among the twelve. And Kyle respected that decision.

"I only need two or three experienced senior men, Armani. You, Coop, T.J., and Fredo are it. You guys watch out for the other seven."

"Roger that. I'm clear on what you need."

"Not what I need. It's what they need. And if they are taken care of, then that's one less thing I have to stress over," Kyle barked.

"You're a liar. You're still going to stress over us all."

"Well, that's on me to bring everyone back safe. And that's what we do, don't we?"

"We certainly do. Thanks, man."

The huge problem with the mission was they also had to accompany two United States senators on this trip. In order to verify and witness the genocide site, it wasn't enough just to collect DNA evidence and send it back to Washington; they wanted an eyewitness, someone who was able to testify at a hearing, to justify what actions were going to be taken by the United Nations and possibly Naval Special Warfare. This task, normally befalling the SEALs, was now being delegated to two U.S. senators, who had never seen combat. Making matters worse, neither one was particularly physically fit.

Their idea of physical fitness was running, like they had perhaps in college, but it had been years since the senators had adopted an exercise routine. With the hot, muggy climate in Western Africa and this being the wet season, the hazards were not only the militant warlords operating in the area, but many different kinds of animals, snakes, reptiles, and insects that could kill them with one bite. Also, working in a hostile environment without a great knowledge of the local languages, customs, or the villages and where they were located, because they moved a lot around the war-torn areas of northern Benin, was a huge disadvantage.

Armando didn't like any bit of it, but he knew Kyle wanted experienced shooters and people who could handle a firefight that could flash up at the last minute and protect the men. It was exactly the kind of mission that he needed at this stage in his life. He was hoping the stress would squeeze out all his negativity and let himself arise from the ashes with a brand-new mindset.

The instant he stepped on the transport plane his military brain kicked into gear. He had never counted the number of missions they'd been on, the number of times they've been jammed up against each other in those buckets of bolts, riding across the Atlantic, making the three or four or five puddle jumps to get to where they needed to be. Thank God they didn't have to do a HALO jump. There was not going to be any quick and cushy helicopter rides inserting them into the jungle at the right spot. Or perhaps the wrong spot, as was wont to happen lately.

Now, they had to do it the old-fashioned way just like soldiers used to do it in Vietnam. They had to cross a variety of paddies, jungles, forge rivers and flash rivers and small lakes. They'd hike through openly hostile villages and seemingly friendly villages, bug-infested killing fields and predator sites. They'd pass dead carcasses of farm animals, slaughtered civilians, and the general detritus of the things that didn't go well in that part of the world. How these people still managed to smile while the children played with their wooden toys, carved stone toys, their rocks, sets of tin cans, their homemade knives, their slingshots, sharp sticks, or sharpened pieces of aluminum that could even be a weapon that might save their lives. A window frame from a blown-up school could become a weapon. A piece of glass wound with strips of animal leather and an abandoned oil drum could help a small child be safe for a short period of time. Youngsters in this region were schooled since they could walk and talk how to defend themselves.

But it was what it was, and the two beefy senators were good sports, but had no idea what they were going to get in the middle of. Hence, instead of bringing two medics in a team of twelve, Kyle chose to bring four—two of them could do backup and operate comms while a couple were designated experts and could fill in where needed for the shooters.

As usual, the information was sketchy. The State Department was not very encouraging, and it was almost as if they were trying to talk them out of going in the first place. Armando knew well the look of a bureaucrat about to possibly send men to their deaths. And he knew that after years of doing this, that it exacted a toll on them, just like it did the men who actually had to fight. He could smell the fear in their bodies, saw the sweat running down under their arms, and tried not to attach too much significance to it or it would eat his brain alive. Details were vague and several of the staff who briefed them and their crew before they took off would not look them in the eyes.

But Kyle did. He made sure he had direct eye contact with all twelve of his men, and Armando knew it was important to keep that contact to make sure he understood that he was there to protect him. Because that was his job. Someone ducking his fierce stare was suspect of having an emotional event, not being prepared, or having doubts. Everyone had doubts, but the trick, Armando knew, was not to show it. He'd gotten very good at it, and it was one of the things about his job, but especially at this time in his journey, he needed to practice doing.

Senator Langley was in his early fifties, the older of the two senators. He was chosen because he served as a backup on the Armed Services Committee. But he also had a contingency of African citizens in the small town just outside of Cincinnati where he had grown up. He had promised mothers and fathers that he would look for relatives; he promised way more than he could produce. He admitted that. He was an honest man, one of the good guys. It was written all over his face. He even wore an American flag wristband with the letters U.S.A. sewn in by hand. Armando guessed it might have been made by one of his family members, perhaps a daughter or his wife.

But Langley would need a lot more than that to survive.

Just like all the rest of the squad.

Armando did respect these two men, no matter how sorely unprepared both were. It took years of battle-tested experience and good intel in order to survive out there. He knew they would both come back to the States forever changed. And not in a good way, either. But Armando's job was to make sure that at least they came back to their wives and their children.

Senator Tosa, barely forty years of age, hailed from Nevada, and was involved with several human rights groups in the Washington D.C. area. He had been a radio announcer in Las Vegas before he ran for Senate. His media presence was savvy, and he knew how to work and manipulate platforms better than most. It helped him gain popularity and get elected—his secret weapon. He was looking forward to some graphic pictures, proof, and evidence to potentially launch an investigation or bring in a UN peacekeeping contingent, to help solve the problem of peace. Everyone knew who the bad guys were. It was bringing back credible proof and galvanizing the public, the government, and the world body to do something to make it stop.

But it was always the same. One hot spot would be taken care of and then another would rise up. People who they once trusted on one mission sometimes changed their colors for the next. And that was the problem. Because nobody from the west lived there full-time, nobody really knew what the temperature was. Even the embassies were clueless. Many of these countries had minimal staff manned by people on their way to a better job.

It was all a guess. They relied on local reports, and sometimes those reports were shaded so that it benefited or aided in the capture or elimination of an enemy. Even though that enemy might not really deserve it.

The airstrip was too short for the size of their plane, which caused the pilots to head down early with a mind-numbing jolt, causing both senators to scream bloody murder.

Armando quickly re-checked their straps and saw that, while they would certainly have welts at their waistband and at the tops of their shoulders, their head did not crack like an egg against the metal ceiling of their transport or damage equipment as they heaved forward after the land.

It was very tight—too tight—but before they deplaned, the pilots turned around in the red, rocky mud path they called an airstrip. The plane nearly got stuck twice, but they had good pilots who were able to keep it going forward, turning it wide, running over stumps of cleared trees and felled brush. Their left wing sliced through the jungle like a hot pair of scissors but caused no apparent damage.

They stopped just long enough to dump the twelve SEALs, their two companions, and all their equipment out the gaping doorway into the mud, and then took off and was gone in less than sixty seconds.

Senator Langley, covered in red clay even on his face after an undignified faceplant, looked around and inhaled, veins at his neck already popping, his white shirt soaking with his own sweat, the mud, and a candy wrapper he'd somehow consumed on the way over.

He winced, and Armando knew full well what he'd picked up. Over in the distance, there was a dead cow, bloated, two legs sticking nearly straight up in the air like a yoga stretch gone very wrong. The stench was overwhelming. None of the SEAL team made any notice of it, but TJ came over to the senator and applied two little tubes of camphor for his nostrils, to keep him from gagging and to keep his airways open.

"You wear these all the time. You wear these until you almost feel naked without them. And you tell me if you get bit by anything. Especially with something that doesn't have legs. You understand?"

"I certainly do," the senator returned.

Armando saw the fear in the gentleman's eyes. So he patted the man on the back. "Don't worry, sir. You'll get used to it eventually. It's not exactly something you're going to want to tell your kids about when you get home, but I think you will kiss the ground as soon as you land there."

Langley displayed a weak smile and nodded.

"You're going to feel like you live like a millionaire when you see how these people live and what they have to put up with. So hang in there. Keep your head down, do what Kyle says, and if you're told to duck, you duck. If you're told to slither on your belly like a snake, you be the best-looking fifty-year-old snake you can make your body do."

The senator stepped back and looked at Armando through the bottoms of his eyes, his lids half closing as if he didn't believe what he'd heard.

Armando knew it was the affectation that caused him to cover up the fact that he was scared to death.

As he should be.

Kyle and Fredo conferred, looked over their GPS units and headed in the direction Kyle pointed. They needed to get to the designated rendezvous with two local UN peacekeepers who braved the wild several miles away to join them. These two were more adept at understanding who the players were and how to get to the site of the horror.

Odinga Uhuru was in his mid-twenties, had been raised in neighboring Nigeria, and had been in college when a skirmish took out most of the area where he had grown up. That included most of his family. He vowed to get even and volunteered, since he was an International Affairs major, to work for the UN in New York where he could serve as an interpreter and help work toward the peace. There, he distinguished himself, and with his knowledge of nearly fifteen local dialects and languages—including German, Russian and some Chinese—he was an integral part to their success even at twenty-five years of age.

Uhuru gave Kyle his version of a street shake, the bump and bang of a local handshake that Kyle had learned on a previous trip. Only Kyle would attempt the movements meant to make white men look ridiculous, even though it didn't take much. Kyle trusted Uhuru, and if Kyle trusted him, Armando did too.

Senator Tosa also attempted to do the handshake but resorted to just sticking his hands out and letting Uhuru make fun of him. He didn't look as awkward because he had more Hollywood in him. His big, white teeth were so bright someone on the Team remarked they could almost use him as a flashlight at night.

Uhuru turned to Senator Langley. "You come all 'dis' way just to get yourself bit and shot? We've already taken pictures, and we told everyone who would listen about this place. I'm not excited that you are here, Senator, but you are, and so we're going to show you what happens when there is no law. When the devil runs the jungle."

Senator Tosa, standing behind Langley, nodded solemnly. Then he swallowed hard. Kyle interrupted the further conversation by asking his UN guide, "So what's the plan then. Do we run straight through tonight or do we wait somewhere and start in the morning? What's your best guess?"

"I think we want to get in quick and get out quick. The idea is to get in before they know you are here and to get out before they have time to organize." Uhuru shook his head. "It's a very nasty trip, especially when we have to book it, only because of the water, which slows us down, and the bugs. We hope and pray that we have no monsoon. If we get a bad storm, we wait. If we don't wait, we drown."

Langley turned to a couple of the SEALs and mumbled under his breath, "So I wonder what the good news is?"

Nobody laughed.

Kyle checked with everyone to make sure all the equipment had arrived. He asked that they check their weapons and ammo, all their scopes, their medical supplies, their maps and extra sets of sterile wipes, repellents, and the tiny medic kits including tourniquets and pills for pain that all SEALs carried now. It was discovered that one of the biggest losses of life was the lack of being able to cut off a bleeder, so every SEAL carried strips that could be used as tourniquets. When you only had thirty seconds to a minute, waiting for a medic was sometimes not an option.

Armando double-checked two of the new shooters, discussed with them what they were carrying, how they were carrying it, adjusted where they carried their sidearm or removed items from their pockets, distributing it better so they could slither on the ground or crawl into a hole. "You want to make sure all your ammo is in a Velcro pocket. Those are fast and easy to get. But you don't want to leave a trail behind you as you're trying to wind your way through the jungle. And if we have to climb a tree, you're going to have to take your breastplate out and put it on your back quickly."

The men had been told this before, and each of them acknowledged his suggestion.

Kyle barked orders, "Okay, gents, we're going to go pretty fast here while we can, and then when it turns dark, we're going to slow down but we're going to keep moving. Uhuru seems to think we might be able to make it there by tomorrow afternoon, but as you know, the enemy gets a vote, and so does that bitch, Mother Nature."

The heat grew even as the sun was beginning to set. Normally, back in the States, there would be some relief as it got dark, but here, that's when all the predators came out. It was also the time when most of the local militia, who were now armed with night vision scopes and other pieces of equipment they didn't have ten or fifteen years ago, thanks to the spread of international arms dealers, would do their trolling.

Most of them were in the child slavery business, the easiest way to make money in these parts. Young women and children could be stolen, hauled away, and forced to make entry into other countries like the UK, Europe, or the United States. Some arrived by boat, but others came through the long porous border with Mexico where manpower was thin and American laws encouraged the traffic.

It was a human chain of tears, a traffic jam that had been going on for several hundred years now and had no chance of stopping. The money they earned even eclipsed the drug trade, considered much more dangerous.

The variegated foliage was shiny and wet with rain. They were instructed to put on their night vision scopes, both senators having been fitted with a pair as well. It was hoped that it would stop the older men from stumbling, but the senators needed frequent help getting over rotted trees or through monkey lakes and rivulets. They both wore traditional hiking shoes, which was the first thing Armando was going to try liberate them from. He wanted to fit them with a regular pair of military boots, if he could find some. They needed something that laced halfway up to their knees, not something that had an edge around the bottom of their ankles. That was extremely dangerous and should have been caught before they boarded the plane.

It was hard pushing, but at last, Uhuru came to a small village he knew, and they quickly ducked into a warehouse-type building that had been made of cement block with a tin roof. No sooner had they gotten themselves inside, then rain started pouring down on the tin roof.

Everyone chose a spot, but they were asked to stay together, not to disperse in the building. Their body heat could help each other, and if something had to be non-verbally communicated, they could do so by the touch of a hand.

Before long, Armando drifted off to sleep. He was dreaming about Gina. The last night they spent together, the wonderful evening when they found each other again, after it was almost thrown away. He remembered how he felt in the hospital, so sure that some miracle would happen, and she would come back to him and prove them all wrong. They'd always weathered the storm—all of them. He felt they always would.

But that didn't happen. And so, Armando slept alone trying to think of his beautiful Gina safe, healthy, and out of pain.

And smiling up at him as he kissed her good night.

CHAPTER 13

S AMBRA TOOK THE advice from several of the SEAL wives, joining a support group for women who had lost husbands, brothers, fathers, or sons in the military. The group was facilitated by a young student named Alice, who she later discovered was an intern working on getting her license and being monitored by Dr. Brownlee.

The room they met in was at a church downtown in Coronado. The Spanish-style building was connected to several other wings with adobe archways and columns covered in ivy. Even though it was late in the year, small birds had nested throughout the courtyards, and their chirping echoed up and down the outside walkways, nearly drowning out the sound of local traffic. The room was set up in a semicircle; couches, chairs, benches, and even a couple futons and exercise balls made up the circle. She noted that just about everyone in the group was double her age or more, but they were very welcoming to her as several came up to ask if she wanted coffee or water, and she felt at home quickly.

She'd decided not to share anything about herself the first time she went, but that was shattered when the group's facilitator asked her to introduce herself and why she wound up in the group.

"Well, I am Sambra Gunnerson, and I lost my husband about three months ago on a mission. He was in the Navy, a SEAL."

"Welcome," the group said in unison.

She darted a look at the facilitator. "Is this some kind of twelve step program or something? I—"

"No! No, that's just what we do. Our form of greeting as a group." The facilitator smiled and asked her to continue.

"We were married over a year, almost a year and a half. We have no children, and I'm not very close to his parents or my own. They all live out of state." She considered saying more but decided against it.

"Welcome, Sambra. We're glad you're here. And if you want to put your name and phone number on the list that's going around, if you ever need someone to talk to, you'll have of a list of all of these ladies here, available to you. Just take one of the copies at the bottom, and you'll be all set. If you need a ride, you need help, or you're needing to speak to someone, even if it's in the middle of night, we've all agreed to help each other. Or to make sure that we get the help we need. There are no rules except that we don't discuss items mentioned in this room outside."

Several of the women immediately welcomed her, and those that hadn't spoken before indicated to her how long they had been without their loved ones. Sambra's recent tragedy was the newest by many months.

After the meeting, Alice invited her to a number of other groups that either she or Dr. Brownlee led, by handing her another list of dates, times, and locations. "These are free and not open to the general public, as we reserve them for military families. But you are welcome anytime you feel comfortable. It will take you a bit to find your home group."

"I don't believe I've met Dr. Brownlee," Sambra said. "I did meet Cooper and Libby, however, but I really haven't had time to connect with most of the team or their wives."

"Well, that surprises me," said Alice. "Normally, they almost make a pest of themselves. It's hard not to stay connected."

"Oh, you mean the casseroles?" Sambra contained a smile by putting her fingers over her mouth. "I stopped those recently. There's only so much tuna noodle you can eat, right?"

Alice giggled and nodded her head. "Well, it sounds like you're dealing with your life with small, careful steps. You're figuring it out. There's a time when you need that closeness, and there's a time when you need to be on your own. You seem like the kind of person who enjoys making her own adventures. And you're so young, that's so unusual."

"I've had a rocky start, I must admit. Erik was perhaps the first person I really trusted, and now I'm starting all over. I don't know what that looks like now."

"You will. In time. It all takes time."

Sambra trusted this young woman, taking the sheet of workshops from her and agreeing to check them out.

"You'll find a group that suits you the best. It might be this one, or it could be a co-ed group. But try to come to something at least once a week. You'll create some consistency that way, and you'll start making friends and develop things that you can build on for your future."

She thought about the immigration attorney. "Actually, I started a venture I never thought I would."

"What's that?" Alice asked.

"I'm adopted. My parents were originally from Syria. But as a toddler, I was brought to the States and adopted. I've recently begun researching my family history. And I've discovered that I may have a brother."

"That's fabulous!" Alice said. "How did you manage to find all this out?"

"I found an immigration attorney who specializes in reuniting family members here with those of their family of origin. And I'm kind of excited, because in two days, I'm going to meet a man who very well could be my brother, whom I've never met before."

"I think that's a wonderful story. And I hope your reunion is everything you wish it to be."

SAMBRA READIED HERSELF for her trip to Los Angeles to meet with the attorney and her long-lost brother. She was filled with excitement. She wore a new dress that she'd purchased the day before, had had her hair cut, and took extra time to apply makeup, giving her eyes a wide expression by using the dark pencil. She liked the result.

On the way in to Los Angeles, she listened several news reports, until she tired of the psycho-babble, and turned on some soothing music for the remainder of the trip. She knew right where she wanted to park, next to the restaurant, and she lightly skipped down the alleyway to the back, the aroma of cooked foods almost celebrating the fact that she was going to be reunited with someone that was of her bloodline.

Inside the attorney's office, she waited behind a closed door where Assad was speaking with someone else. She was early so perused the office magazine rack for interests the attorney might have. Nothing stood out to her.

Then Assad opened the door and gave her a wide grin. "My dear, it is my extreme pleasure to introduce you to someone who is from your family. This is Khalil, and he has come to Los Angeles expressly to meet you, Sambra."

A tall, very thin man of about thirty stood timidly in the doorway, his chin and eyes downcast in a slight bow. As his eyes rose to meet hers, he gave her another, deeper bow, mumbling some greeting she knew to be Arabic. He acted very shy, as if speaking to her was causing him some embarrassment.

Sambra could see that from his affectations that he was not raised in Western culture. He seemed hesitant to step forward and shake hands, even though she had extended hers.

"It's nice to meet you Khalil. I'm Sambra. And Assad tells me you are my brother."

"Yes, Sister, I am your brother. And it is a great day to be able to make your acquaintance."

His shyness lingered, still uncomfortable being in her presence.

"So have you traveled from Syria, or where have

you been living?" she asked him.

"I have come from Paris," he said with a soft voice. "I have lived the last five years in Paris, attending school."

His formal response to her question was not what she expected, but she knew the cultural differences in how they'd been raised were very strong.

"Khalil and Sambra, I want to invite you both to my home this evening for dinner. My wife and I will cook for you some of our favorite items. Everything will be homemade." He grinned. "Khalil, you need to know that Sambra is not accustomed to our foods."

The young man's eyes grew wide. "Oh really? That's unfortunate. Then we shall teach you, Sambra."

She studied both these men in front of her. It was so different than what she expected, but she embraced it as much as she could take in. "I'm looking forward to it. I promise I shall be a loyal and good sister to you, brother. I have so many things I wish to ask you. And we have much catching up to do, don't we?"

"Indeed."

"Do you know where our parents are, or if they are living?" she asked him.

"Now, Sambra, give your brother a chance. Not only has he met his sister, but I'm afraid your beauty and grace has got him tongue-tied." The attorney rocked back on his heels and gave a deep chuckle.

"But I have so many questions, Mr. Nefrusia. We may have other living relatives." She looked around the attorney, querying Khalil. "Do we?"

He began to answer when Assad interrupted him. "No. I insist. We treat this like a real family reunion. First, we meet. Then we drink and dine. We celebrate the connections once lost, now found. And that is the time for the answers to your questions, my dear. All your questions will be revealed. But come, child. Let's gather at my home."

Sambra heard Khalil speak to the attorney in Arabic, and after a brief discussion, Assad outstretched his arms, first turning to Khalil.

"Khalil, you will drive with me in my car, and, Sambra, you will follow?"

"Khalil, you may ride with me, if you like. I'm a good driver," she said to him.

Her brother's brow furled, and he stepped back into Assad's office, as if needing protection of some kind.

"He's not used to women driving. That is not possible in Syria. So you must give him a little bit of time to get used to it here."

"I thought he's spent part of his life in Paris. Surely women drive there," she challenged.

"Patience, Sambra. You must have patience. You have all the time in the world to get acquainted and to perhaps meet others of your family. I'm sure Khalil will enjoy accompanying you any place you would like, but first, we celebrate! I insist!" The attorney gave her another grin, and that was the end of that.

She agreed and said so.

But Assad Nefrusia did remind Sambra of the Cheshire cat in her favorite story as a child, lovingly read to her by her mother:

Alice in Wonderland.

CHAPTER 14

A T LAST, AND while it was still the hot part of the day around noon, Uhuru and his second slowed the pace down.

"It's getting close," Uhuru said.

He sent Abel on ahead to scout for evidence of militia or recently used camps. He explained that often militia groups guarded these sites of atrocities, knowing that there would be interest from the Western world. And that's how they'd pick up either family members coming to grieve or international press or aid workers, who they might be able to capture and hold for ransom.

"We had a group from Belgium, nurses and some doctors, coming in to help after such a massacre at one of our local schools. All of them were captured and held. You probably don't hear about it in your press, but one by one, they're being released. Two have died. It's been over three years now."

Armando was sickened by that news. He could see the senators were greatly moved as well. He chose this space to make a point he'd been wanting to make for some time.

"These guys…" He pointed to the SEAL members of the squad. "These guys are here to make sure that does not happen. I want you to understand, they put their lives on the line for you. And you must repay them by doing your job, being smart, and not getting in their way. Do you understand?"

That forced an additional comment from their U.N. keepers. "Senators, hired by the people of the United States, do you hear this man? He's talking serious now. He's talking about you two."

Uhuru's command of leadership was extraordinary, Armando thought. At twenty-five years of age, he was a keen judge of character, a person who could be trusted with information. He also appeared to be unafraid of the dangers all around him.

Senator Langley spoke softly. "I promise you, Uhuru, your story will be told. I will make sure even the president himself gets this information. And I salute your bravery and your commitment."

"Nah." Uhuru laughed and shook his head from side to side, trying to appear casual. "You would do the same if you had nothing left." He followed it up with a raging cackle that put Armando's nerves on edge.

There wasn't a single soul in the group who would even dare give him a reply.

They continued at half the pace they were before, and luckily, the terrain was slightly easier. It looked to Armando like the fields had at one time been farmed, and there were remnants of cattle pens and small huts. But most of anything that was made of wood was burned or used for firewood, and nothing remained of the village that was probably located here. It would take a year, but the jungle would return, and it would look like nothing ever existed in this spot.

As they got closer to the site, Uhuru slowed them down even further. He asked everyone to search each step, turning to examine the brush around them, to report if they saw any evidence of people or vehicles, weapons, or some kind of a stash house or building that could store weapons.

True to his word, Armando searched the surrounding jungle on the right. On the left was a lake bordered in red mucky clay, frequented by animals judging from the footprints he found there. In the middle of the lake was a dead zebra.

"Predators," Uhuru said, pointing to the zebra.

Abel met them on their path about a half an hour later and reported that the site appeared to be abandoned for the present time, but he said he heard villagers in the distance, perhaps a few miles away.

Armando was aware of how voices sometimes carried in dense forests, making estimation of distance difficult.

Abel continued. "Boss," he addressed Uhuru, "I think we have some villagers coming to sort through the bodies. So we need to do what we do and get out quickly. They are going to cause commotion."

"Good idea," said Kyle.

Uhuru agreed, followed closely behind Abel with the rest of the team moving through the forest in a group, so that the SEALs could run point on the outsides, protecting the senators in the middle.

Uhuru had an antiquated Russian rifle, but Abel was only armed with a spear. Armando suspected that, in one of his pockets, he may have carried a handgun of some kind. But with a Grateful Dead t-shirt and khaki shorts, homemade flip flops made from animal leather straps, he looked more like an overgrown teenager out hunting. Armando figured that was by design.

At a break in the foliage, Armando could smell the bodies before he saw them. He motioned for the senators to put a kerchief over their mouth and nose for the smell. T.J. gave Langley another couple of nose tubes.

Both men stood at the edge of the abyss with the SEALs to the side. It was just like a medieval oil painting of what hell might look like. Bodies were bloated and strewn across a section of ground about the width of a soccer field. Some bodies were cut down as they had tried to climb up out of the pit. He suspected they had all been forced in there and then were either murdered by machete-wielding militia or shot from the edges. But the wounds were made with heavy blades or axes, spears, a few arrows, and many, many gunshot wounds to the head. It was indiscriminately laid out, children, even babies in their mothers' arms, old women, old men, and a few youths.

Armando noticed one exception to the pile of bodies. There did not appear to be very many young women. He knew exactly why.

"Holy shit. I'm going to be sick." Langley gasped and quickly ducked back into the bushes to vomit. Tosa's face, normally handsome and well-tanned, laugh lines so prominent and attractive, looked white, shocked, like he was literally having a heart attack. TJ watched him closely and whispered something to him. Tosa stepped aside and threw his arms in the opposite direction.

The man was embarrassed that he felt so much repulsion and rage.

"I just need a minute. I just need one minute." And then he burst into tears.

"So we're going to stand here and cry over people

who don't even know we're here? Or are we going to get this job done and get back to safety?" Uhuru asked.

Armando didn't particularly like his tone, but he chalked it up to fear and knowledge that this was but a brief reprise between volleys of sudden death encounters, carnage, grief, and horror. He offered to help Tosa with carrying any of his equipment and was turned down.

"I got it. Let me just get my drone out—"

"Hold it. Wait just one minute!" Kyle said. "What are you doing there?"

"I'm preparing the drone, so I can take a camera shot of the whole place. From a drone, I'll be able to really show what's here," Tosa explained.

"I didn't approve any drone shots. And I abso-fucking-lutely don't approve of you taking pictures of my team. That is not going to happen. And if you do, I will take your camera, and I will personally break it myself." Kyle was livid.

"I can take stills from the drone. But it will be more effective if I can get the whole scene, Lansdowne. You have to understand, in order to make a point, to prove that this happened, we have to orient the viewers to what is really here. They see bodies all the time. They don't see bodies in piles that look like this." Tosa nodded to the horrific scene to his left.

Uhuru stepped in front of Kyle, separating him

from the senator. "If you think about it, what he's here to do is to help drum up support. We've already told everybody about what's going on here. But I'm just a young African man. I could be lying, right? They don't listen to me at your Senate hearings. But them, Senator Tosa, Senator Langley? They'll be all over this shit. You need to let him take some pictures that will make people do what Langley just did. We want them to vomit and shit their pants."

Uhuru's jaw was firm, his eyes menacing, laser-focused on Kyle.

"Okay, so this is how it's gonna roll. You all need to get your stuff together. Drink some water, and get ready for the quick return. I want to get us out of here in…" Kyle checked his watch. "I want to get us out of here in five to ten minutes max. Tosa, you get your drone up in the air, and I'm going to check all the footage before you go sharing it on the internet. You can do one big sweep, one video. But if I see any of my men in any of those pictures, I'm going to erase that film. So I'm being flexible here."

Langley and Tosa stepped up beside Uhuru, who had been defending them. Tosa said, "I'm good with that, Kyle. I'm not going to push the envelope."

Tosa took out his tiny drone, attached a mini video camera to it, and then set the thing flying. It was absolutely noiseless, and Tosa directed it with an app on his cell phone, which had been given to him by the State Department, so they could locate him and Langley at all times.

"Would you look at that?" said Fredo, admiring the small, winged projectile.

"Boy, that makes my drone look like an old jalopy, a Model T or something," said Coop.

"Yeah," Tosa called back over his shoulder. He was biting his lower lip. "I got these little things from one of my buddies at the CIA. They got all kinds of shit there. It's kind of a maiden voyage for them. Kills two birds with one stone in a way."

Kyle and Armando stood with their hands on their hips scanning the foliage around them. Armando knew Kyle was just as nervous as he was. He kept checking his watch.

"We got about three minutes left Tosa. And I mean it about those pictures. I better not even see the legs of my men."

Uhuru turned to Kyle, placing his hands on his shoulder. "You got to relax, my man. Just give him a chance."

Kyle stared back at him and pushed the African's hands to the side. "We spent a lot of time getting trained here, working up for this deployment. We put our asses on the line all the time. I've worked my way up through the ranks, and I've gotten a lot of men home safe. That's what I'm going to continue to do. But I'll be damned if I make one stupid move. If I allow him to take a picture that puts one of my guys on social media, all of a sudden, what do we have? We have somebody who's going to claim we did this. So you better not aid the enemy by doing that. I just want to get home, and I don't want to lose my career over some Hollywood-type who wants to make a name for himself. This is not the nightly news. We're fucking with people here who don't have any good intentions for you, you, you or you." He pointed to everybody.

"And that's a fact," Armando said, standing right next to him. "You can take that to the bank, boys. We aren't here to put the Navy, our teammates, the SEAL program, or special warfare program in the crosshairs of anybody's pet peeve. And there's a lot of people out there that would feel a whole lot safer if we weren't here with you guys. So cool it."

Coop looked at Armando and started to chuckle.

"He is back," Fredo said.

"Ain't that the fucking truth," agreed Coop. "Glad to see it, Armani. I'm real glad to have you back."

Just as Tosa was reeling in his drone, they heard voices coming through the brush, and a few women in multicolored skirts and sarongs made it to the edge of the huge crater of bodies. Tosa turned to Kyle.

"One picture?"

"Shit. One or two, make it quick. We got to disappear."

Abel was nodding whispering something to Uhuru.

Uhuru nodded back and told Kyle, "Abel says these are ladies from the village that they raided. He was told that their daughters were missing, and they came to the pit to see if they could find them."

"You see any young women in that hole?" asked TJ.

"Not one. I don't see one," said Uhuru.

"It's a damn shame," said Fredo.

Without being noticed, the team extracted back into the jungle. Fredo had been in communication with the birds upstairs, and he ordered a big bird to pick them up. He informed them that, so far, they had fourteen, since Uhuru and Abel wanted to come with them. He also let them know that no one was injured as of yet.

Armando heard the squawking in Fredo's earpiece, confirming the order.

"You can follow Langley's GPS? Is that correct?"

More squawking on the other end had Fredo nodding his head yes to Kyle.

"So we'll be at the clearing, at those coordinates, unless something changes, close to midnight. You cool with that?"

Again, the squawking on the comms alerted everyone. Tosa was re-packing his equipment, checking his batteries, and then stowing everything for their march through the brush.

Fredo shook his head violently back and forth. "No can do, sir. That ain't going to happen."

After more squawking, Fredo let out a string of expletives.

"Damn it all to hell. They want us to find some place to hunker down for the night, and then they'll pick us up in the morning. What about an 'emergency extraction' don't they understand?"

Kyle was a little more lenient with the news. "Fredo, you don't know what they got going. And now we're carrying fourteen instead of twelve. So maybe they got an equipment issue. But you're never going to know. And they don't want to lose that bird. You know that. For whatever reason, we're going to have to do what we do. Uhuru, should we go back to the warehouse?"

Their U.N. guide shook his head. "I think we're going to have to find a new place to make camp. But let's get out at the crack of dawn. How much notice you got to give?" he asked Fredo.

"Thirty minutes. Now that I know they're looking for us, they'll know where we are, and they might redirect us someplace else. But you try to find us a landing somewhere big enough for one of those Black Hawks, and we'll be out of here as soon as they land. I don't think they want to come in the middle of the day. My guess is dawn is the optimum time."

"Roger that then," said Kyle. "You lead the way, son. And thanks for getting us here."

Langley was still white and vomiting every few feet. He was in close contact with TJ and Coop, who were both monitoring his condition. He answered all of their medical questions, and since any other condition was ruled out, Coop just stated the obvious.

Whispering into Armando's ear, he said, "He's just shook up. Nothing wrong with it, man. Just going to go home with a new set of values, I think. Some new things to keep him awake at night. Just like you and me, Armani."

CHAPTER 15

AWN BEGAN TO peek through the foliage around the perimeter of the former garden of a wealthy landowner—at least they'd been wealthy at one time. Now the enormous stone house was cratered with mortar holes and cave-ins. Fires had ravaged the surrounding farmland, but at one time, this was probably a beautiful, bucolic home of a wealthy farmer, perhaps even a warlord. They even saw an old plastic playhouse, a tire swing, and an iron spring fashioned into a rocking horse on the side, indicating a family had lived here at one time.

The orange glow on the dome of the sky was ominous. Armando picked up the scent of fire and heard light rounds several miles away. He had boarded a Black Hawk just like this one a number of missions ago in the middle of the night, and he had helped wounded team guys load onto the helicopter with the hoist that was sometimes used.

In this case, the beast was able to land. Within seconds, Kyle directed the team to head for the open doorway, and all of them climbed inside, a couple of the men helping Langley step up inside and giving him space where Cooper could treat some of the cuts he'd sustained running through the brush and falling on sharp rocks. Coop didn't waste any time in cutting off the senator's pants above the knee.

As the helicopter rose to the sky, the senator made a comment about how he was going to have the Navy pay for those pants.

Coop was well known for his wit and putting things into perspective with his Nebraska common sense. He looked up at the senator and said, "Just be glad you've got legs that stick out. I've had to cut off pants from people who no longer have legs or feet. You're one of the lucky ones, Senator. These are just scratches, but we don't want them to get infected, because they're super nasty."

Armando checked Kyle's expression and noted that his LPO was about to burst into a chuckle that would probably not be appropriate.

Tosa was clicking through some of the shots he'd taken of the site. "Damn, these are better than I thought. No question about what this is. The detail is almost too good."

Armando knew exactly what he meant.

"Well then, we'll call it a success," he said to the senator.

"Hold on. I'm going to take a look at those as soon as we get back to Germany," Kyle said. "I'm not leaving you alone until I get a chance to cull through those pictures. And I mean it about erasing those that are not going to be appropriate."

"I understand completely."

Tosa sported a completely flat expression.

The pilot tapped on Kyle's shoulder. "I have no instructions on them. I'm returning them to Germany, is that right, or do we have to make a pit stop on the way?"

Armando knew these Black Hawk pilots were known to be rather cheeky, and they were the best of their kind. Absolutely one hundred percent solid, able to be counted on in any situation.

"Gee, that's funny, I was told you were going to escort them all the way back to D.C. I guess I'm going to have to get with the head shed and complain about some of these instructions." Kyle laughed.

They were transported to an airfield and then flown back to Germany, where Uhuru and Abel planned to meet up with a U.N. delegation.

"You're going to email me some of those pictures, Senator?" Uhuru asked Tosa.

"Absolutely. Here, you put your email in my

phone, and I'll make sure I get it to you as soon as I get clearance to release it. And thanks, man."

Kyle addressed Uhuru. "I'm real impressed with you, son. You ever want to do anything with the Navy again, you just let me know. Are you interested in citizenship?"

"I might be. But I got family over there still. If it would mean help getting them out, yeah, I'd be interested. Abel here has family, as well. I'd like to help him too."

Kyle shook both of their hands, this time without the local shake, and expressed gratitude, as did the rest of the team.

Armando followed Kyle and Coop and the rest of the squad, including the two senators down to the transport area so they could be delivered to their liaison office. They had a team building in Germany, but it was shared by multiple SEAL teams and other Special Forces units. Kyle seemed to be a little more lighthearted as they got closer and closer to safety.

Armando was pleased there were no injuries.

"So where do you want to do this examination?" Senator Tosa asked.

Kyle's face lit up. "I got a place. They serve beer, too, and boy, do I need one."

Senator Langley asked if he could be excused so he could change his clothes, check in with the office, and let everyone know he's back.

Kyle was quick with the permissions. "You do that, sir. We're going to be right down past the freight elevator, over at that yellow building. You see that big banana thing over there?"

Langley acknowledged it.

"We'll be in there. It's air conditioned, and it has a bar."

Tosa let Kyle know that they were on a chartered flight to get back to D.C. together. "So I don't think he's going to wander too far." He shouted to Langley's back. "But you do look kind of messed up, Charlie."

Langley looked at the front of his shirt, turned, and gave him the finger.

"I think he washed that thing three or four times. You never get that dirt out. Never," whispered Armando.

Kyle cocked his head. "I dunno. Orange is kind of a good color for him, don't you think, gents?"

"I think that thing's done for," laughed T.J.

Armando watched him head back through the terminal building. He thought the senator looked like he was ten, maybe twenty years older than when they left.

After they were seated, Tosa brought out his camera and started to play his pictures. Kyle nixed a couple of them. Tosa argued with him a bit, but Kyle was no-nonsense, and if it had a pixel that could identify any body part, fingernail, or tattoo of a Team 3 guy, it was out. And Kyle didn't hesitate to delete the picture, even before he told Tosa he was doing so.

"Geez, Lansdowne, you don't give me very much to work with."

"Hollywood, I think with your good looks and your extensive background in spin, you can make a whole lot out of this material. And I hope you do. I just don't want to let anybody know we were part of it." Kyle smiled, patted him on the back, and said, "Now let's get that beer."

A DAY AND a half later, Armando was back in Coronado. He felt it had been a solid mission. Fortunately, they hadn't had to deal with enemy combatants there, the intel had been good, and their scouts were excellent. It was one of the only times he'd been on a mission without having to fire off a round. All in all, the job was carried out just like they'd planned. They even returned on the date they were supposed to.

Gina would've been pleased with that.

On his way back to his bungalow, he realized it was more than time for him to start attending some grief counseling. He didn't want to go see the woman who had helped them with their marriage counseling, as it brought up too many old wounds and difficult memories. He was ready to face some new realities, and the only one he really trusted was Dr. Brownlee. So he gave him a call, and Austin recommended that he try a group setting first. Afterwards, they'd meet and set up some private appointments later on the next week.

Next on the list was American food—good American food—so he took himself to the finest steakhouse in San Diego, had dinner and a nice glass of red wine, poured garlic mashed potatoes over everything, and then telephoned his mother.

He was going to pick up Artemis and bring him home. He was dying to see his son. But Felicia begged him to go home and get some rest first and pick him up in the morning.

"Oh, Armando. He is having such a wonderful time. I'm afraid we've spoiled him."

"Of course you did, Mom. That's what grandmas do."

"He knows you'll be here. I told him maybe tomorrow, but now I will let him know I've heard from you. He will like that."

"Has he asked about Gina?"

She sighed then the end of the phone was dead quiet. "All the time, my son. He asks about her all the time. But I'm afraid I have to let you take care of the information you want him to have. It's your job. It's something he should hear from his daddy."

"I agree, Mom. Okay then, I'll see you tomorrow. I

got a meeting to go to at ten in the morning, but after that, I'll stop by and pick him up, okay?"

"You got it, Son. Glad you're home safe. I prayed for you the whole time. I hope whatever it is that you were doing, you took care of the bad guys."

"Thanks, Mom." Armando chuckled as he disconnected.

At home, he laid out the clothes he was going to wear tomorrow, his first act of being off duty. That would not have been top of the list if Gina was here, but he had lots of wonderful memories of those reunions and the way she welcomed him back. Tomorrow, though, he was going to turn the page on that, dress up, probably give up drinking for a while, and just try to live. He was going to live for his son.

Everything depended on that.

CHAPTER 16

Assad's home didn't resemble his office downtown at all. The house was sprawling and contained several large sitting rooms. He had a pool in the backyard and an office back there as well. He told Sambra that he had four children, two that were living on their own and two attending college nearby, but they would not be at the house for dinner. He also mentioned he had some friends stopping by, acquaintances of Khalil.

His wife was busying herself in the kitchen, wearing a more traditional dress, but without a head scarf. She was quickly making delicacies, things Sambra had never tasted before. It was elaborately spread out on multiple platters all over the dining room table, and she mentioned that in their family they sat in a circle and ate from these platters or a common pot.

"You take this, you use these crepes—I'm going to call them crepes, because you don't know what they are—and you fill your hands with this delicious food. This is cauliflower, these are chickpeas, and we have eggplant and black mushrooms. Nothing here is overly spicy, but if you like heat, I do have sauces at the other end. Be very careful with the orange one."

She didn't look at Sambra as she gave these instructions. Her tone was respectful and calm. She paid absolutely no attention to Khalil or her husband.

Assad brought out a bottle of wine he had purchased for the occasion. "I presume you drink wine, my dear?"

"I love wine."

Khalil declined to take his. "I don't care for the taste. I'm sorry," he said timidly.

Assad stepped up to him and put his hand against Khalil's cheek. "Good boy. You are a good boy, my son."

Sambra was going to start asking Khalil some questions about their family back in Syria when they heard a knock at the door.

"Ah, your friends, Khalil."

Two older gentlemen walked into the room. The first one, tall and extremely handsome, dressed expensively in a black double-breasted velvet long coat. He appeared to be close to Assad's age but in much better shape. He was polished, his dark eyes dancing back and forth as he almost flirted with Sambra, which caused her to blush out of embarrassment. That brought a smile to his lips.

"I am delighted to meet you, my dear. My name is Ansari Timur, and Assad has told me so much about you. I am so grateful you have invited me and my assistant to this meeting."

"Assad is a most gracious host," the other gentleman said. "I am Fazrah Bonsil. It is our duty as fellow countrymen to make sure you are protected."

"Well, thank you. However, I kind of see myself as an American. I don't see myself as foreign. And I don't think I need protection. I'm learning to navigate quite well on my own. That said, I'm Syrian by birth, but my whole life has been spent here in the United States. This is my home. But I am curious about my family, my culture."

"Indeed. And you will enjoy it a great deal, my dear," Assad said.

"One thing you will find about your fellow countrymen," Ansari said, ignoring Sambra's comment about independence, "is that we tend to be very direct and truthful. I must tell you that a young unmarried woman always is in need of protection. It is one of the things about our culture women enjoy and men insist on."

Sambra felt like a challenge had been leveled at her. "And I will certainly remember that if and when I am ever in need of it." She didn't smile at first, making sure he understood she was dead serious, but then her lips softened, and she presented him with a sweet and very contrite smile.

Ansari Timur's eyes sparkled at the dance of their conversation. "And you are so young to be so wise. Where are your parents?" he asked.

"They live in Portland. I'm afraid we are not close." She knew Timur would never understand any explanation she could give, so she didn't try.

Khalil stood nervously by her side. Before he could offer something, Ansari commented on her dress.

"You look exceedingly beautiful. Doesn't she, Khalil?"

"Yes, I agree."

"And purple is definitely your color." He smiled, and Sambra felt something tighten inside her, something she didn't fully trust.

Assad interrupted. "Most distinguished guests, please will you have some food? I brought wine if you'd like some."

Ansari completely ignored him. Assad quickly left the room.

"Come, Sambra. You and Khalil, come sit with me."

Sambra looked at the second gentleman, the assistant, who was much younger and not quite as polished as Timur.

"Excuse me, but I don't believe we know each other," she started. "Let me introduce myself. I am Sambra Gunnerson." She extended her hand.

The gentleman took her hand in his, and as he did so, his wrist went limp.

Timur clasped his hands together. "There, now you have all met, and now we shall talk." He directed Khalil and Sambra over to a conversation area in the corner of the living room. Mrs. Nefrusia served them hors d'oeuvres and kept bringing wine for Sambra and sparkling water for Khalil and Ansari. She quickly retreated to the kitchen.

Sambra examined the room and didn't see Assad. "Where has Assad gone?"

From the kitchen, Mrs. Nefrusia called out, "He had to run back to the office to pick up something. I think he had to meet somebody there briefly. He will be back, though. Don't worry, Sambra."

"Anyway, we have all this wonderful food here. I'm sure he wouldn't want to miss this feast," said Ansari.

Sambra tasted some of the colorful morsels from her plate. "So what exactly do you do? Are you part of Assad's organization? Do you help him?" she asked. As she looked between the two men, Khalil didn't appear to have an answer forthcoming, nor did he answer. The other gentleman, Fazra, didn't appear to understand the question in the first place.

She was beginning to realize that Khalil, Assad's wife, and Fazra were all foreign born, but she deduced Ansari and Assad had spent significant time in the U.S., if not raised here.

She continued. "Do you work here in the Los Angeles area?"

"I work all over the U.S. I travel a great deal."

She nodded. "And Khalil, where are my—our parents? Are they still alive? And are there others of my family alive, and where do they live?"

Khalil had begun to answer, but Ansari cut him off.

"So many questions, my dear." Ansari's eyes flashed as he lovingly scanned her new dress. "First to your question about what I do. I am a facilitator. What I do is I work for various groups in this country who wish to sponsor refugees. In most cases, these are not children like your situation. These are individuals who are in search of learning, a cultural exchange, or intellectual pursuits. They're usually college age or young adult age. We aren't in the business of bringing in family units, but we are interested in fostering understanding between our two cultures. Don't you agree that if people know each other better, it's easier to get along?"

Sambra agreed with that completely. "Yes. I think fostering more understanding is the best way to solve issues and problems. It's hard when we have so much distance between our two countries."

"Exactly. I couldn't have said it better myself."

"So our family… I mean, are you my brother, Khalil?"

"Yes, Sister. I am your brother, by family and by blood. Most definitely."

"How did you come to live in Paris then?"

"Our family sent me there, along with my younger brother. Yes, you had another brother, who unfortunately has gone to Heaven. It was thought to be much more safe for the two of us, so I came to Paris, and we lived together until his demise."

"I'm so sorry. Was he ill?"

"It was an accident. A horrible accident. But I was spared."

"Sambra, there are a few things you need to understand. First of all, we are opposed to the wholesale transportation of our children to other countries, especially for the purpose of integrating them into the host country's society. Khalil spent most of his youth in Syria. But these last few years he was in Paris, training at an art school. He is a magnificent artist. Aren't you, Khalil?"

Khalil nodded profusely. "Yes, yes. I love my art."

"I'd very much like to see your work," Sambra answered. "I myself cannot draw anything." She followed it up with a nervous laugh.

Ansari added, "As for your family, my dear, unfortunately for your parents, all of the older generation are gone, but there are several nieces and nephews of your family, as well as Khalil. We believe there is another brother too. You are fortunate in that you were given American citizenship. Khalil does not have this."

As Sambra let that sink in, questions arose. "So you're asking for my help to get him citizenship?"

"Well, maybe eventually." Ansari seemed to slough it off as if it was an afterthought. "The main thing is that you meet each other, and you open the door to meeting the rest of your family too."

"I would very much like to. Okay, Khalil, you are living in Paris, so you will go back to Paris then? And when?"

"I would like to—"

Ansari interrupted him once again. "He has been accepted at U.C. San Diego. Isn't that correct, Khalil?"

"Yes, I just received the notification this week. And we are making the arrangements necessary."

"That's great news. We will be close then. We can meet and get together. I can show you Southern California. I know a lot about the San Diego area, but I've also been up north in wine country, and I was raised in Oregon. I can tell you a lot about the United States, particularly the West Coast."

"That would be wonderful. I look forward to it, Sister."

Ansari Timur watched their interaction very carefully. A smile never left his face. He listened to the back and forth between brother and sister. And he seemed to approve.

"Ansari, back to my other questions. What exactly do you do with these groups? Is it like a cultural club?" she asked.

"Very much so. We are a social club like many of your immigrant groups are. We advocate for representation so that our culture is protected from misunderstandings. It's a chance for young people of our lineage to meet. I help young students such as Khalil get comfortable, situated. And young people such as you, it's a chance for you to get acquainted with your past. I think this will be a marvelous experiment and a wonderful experience for you. I can see that you have a hunger for the culture so carelessly ripped from your grip. That was so unfair, and we hope and pray we can remedy that."

That set off a red flag in Sambra's gut. Assad's return to the living room turned the conversation toward their dinner.

Sambra stayed the whole evening, without having a private, one-on-one conversation with Khalil. Either Assad or Ansari always interfered. But she knew that it would take a while before she would feel comfortable. These things took time, and she resigned herself to be patient. The main thing was she had now been given another path to follow, if she chose to. She hoped her questions would be more fully explored and resolved in time.

As she said goodbye and drove home, she wondered what kind of a box she had opened. One thing was for certain, though, her life after tonight was never going to be the same. She was beginning a new page, a new chapter in her life. Her old story was going to be left behind forever.

CHAPTER 17

ARMANDO SHOWED UP at the small meeting room located in Dr. Brownlee's office complex. He was the first one to arrive. Brownlee was organizing chairs, setting some literature on the tables nearby and had started brewing some coffee.

"Ah, Armando. That's a very welcoming sign, to have you be the first one here. I am delighted." He took three long strides to shake Armando's hand.

"Well, we got back yesterday, and I decided I'd just jump right in. I hope I'm dressed presentably."

"Most times I've seen you, you usually wear those slip-ons, khaki shorts, and T-shirts with all those crazy skull drawings on it. I'm glad you didn't do that today. Although this crowd, mostly military people and their spouses, would probably understand it. But it's always not a good idea to scare the audience at your first performance." Dr. Brownlee winked at him.

Armando searched the room looking for something to do. "So what's left?"

"Let's see. I think in the kitchen there are some foam cups, and there's a little half-and-half left in the refrigerator. Maybe you could set that out next to the coffee maker and see if they managed to throw out the sugar. It's a long running battle I've had with several of my colleagues about serving sugar when coffee is actually the more important drug here."

Armando chuckled, "Well, that's a conversation I've never heard, and frankly, I don't pay attention to it. If I like it, I eat it. If I don't, I don't. And I figure if I have to, I'll just work a little harder if it has side effects. It works for alcohol, and I think it works for sugar too."

"Be careful of the alcohol, though."

"You know, I forgot to mention to you that I'm going to swear off drinking for about thirty days. I just decided I'd try it. Ever since I made it to the Teams, it's just been so much a part of our culture. Not getting drunk like I have done recently, I'm not happy to say, but the beers, you know, the beers every night with a hamburger and the French Fries. I'm just going to lay low of that stuff for a while, and see what that does to me."

"Excellent idea."

Brownlee looked up and greeted several people who had gathered in the doorway.

"Come. Come on in. Help yourself to coffee, please."

Three military-aged men and two women entered the room, passing by Armando on their way to the coffee pot. One of the ladies brought some cookies under tinfoil on a tray. Armando raised his eyebrows to take a look.

"You like chocolate chip?" she asked.

Armando looked at Dr. Brownlee before he answered. "Who doesn't, but yes, I do, and I'm probably going to have too many this morning. If you don't mind."

"Not at all," she said, as she brought the tray over to him. "Take your pick."

Armando noticed her red nail polish, which was the color Gina had loved, noticed her pretty pink skin, and the lack of a wedding ring on her left hand. He was only guessing, but he thought perhaps she was a widow. He wasn't going to pry.

"Thank you, ma'am."

She gave a pert smile, turned, and set the cookies on the table. She adjusted the coffee maker, the napkins, the sugar, and the cups so it was balanced, took her ponytail down, and then put her hair back up in a clip. Her light auburn hair set off her peachy complexion. She was not beauty queen beautiful, but her features were wholesome and solid. And she had a nice smile. Armando pulled himself away, reminding himself to take things slow.

As he sat next to Dr. Brownlee, others drifted into the room. He lost track of the count, but it appeared to be mostly populated with military-aged men or fathers and mothers. There were only a few women present.

Dr. Brownlee introduced himself as he closed the door and flipped the sign to the outside to "Private" and returned to his chair.

"I know most of you know the drill, but today is the first day for some of you here. And I would like you to give us a brief introduction, what brings you here, and what you hope to accomplish today? Let's start with you, Armando. I have to tell the room that Armando serves on a SEAL Team that a relative of mine, a very close relative of mine, has married into. Is that the right way to put it?" He frowned and looked at Armando, who shrugged.

"His daughter married one of my teammates, okay?"

Brownlee winced. "Okay, we're not supposed to say that, but now that it's out there, that's the case. And, Armando, do you want to tell us what brings you here?"

All of a sudden Armando felt very much on the spot, unsure of what he wanted to say. He didn't know these people, and it was not like he or any of the SEAL

Team guys opened up without knowing who they were opening up to. It was just a thing they never did.

"My wife was a police officer when I met her, and we fell in love. She had taken a break when we found out we were going to have a baby. She took several years off and had just recently decided to go back on the force."

He had to take several slow, tactical breaths to level his nerves before he could continue.

"Unfortunately, on her very first day back at work, she was involved in a traffic accident, and she was killed. I'm recovering, that was about four weeks ago now, and since then I have even done a quick deployment with my team. I'm not here today as a SEAL, I'm here so I can feel normal. I just want to be normal. I don't want to be a man who's lost his wife. I don't want to be a SEAL who's just come back from a mission and is damaged. I just want to live. I want to find out who I really am and what I'm going to do with the rest of my life."

Dr. Brownlee placed his palm on Armando's knee. Turning his face, he spoke to him. "That's a hell of a start, Son. I'd say you've done a lot of work."

"I'm not sure I did anything, Doctor. I think just doing what I do, doing what I actually love to do, is the best kind of medicine. The problem for me is when I'm not there—on the job."

He heard a couple members of the group sniffle. Somebody blew their nose, and he heard the cookie lady sigh, uttering in a whisper, "Wow."

Dr. Brownlee stood up and paced back and forth in the center of the circle. "I have to say something firsthand. I probably haven't revealed too much in this group; I make it a habit not to reveal too much to my patients either, but here goes."

Brownlee's solid frame slowly shifted from balancing on his right and then his left leg. He rubbed his hands together. Armando suspected he was not sure about the wisdom of his share.

"I had a twin brother who became a Navy SEAL."

He circled the room, his hands now on his hips, looking into the faces of everyone present. Armando watched his casual demeanor, his lithe athletic body, even at his sixty-something age. He hoped he would look as good when he reached that age one day.

"I had a good life, a family, and recently, I lost my wife as well. Most of you know that."

Many in the audience nodded their heads.

"But what you probably don't know is that my twin brother, Will, didn't come home. We lost him in Grenada. And I wasn't capable of understanding the kind of sacrifice he had put himself through. Our family wasn't sympathetic to anything military, really. I'd seen too much pain and suffering, too much mismanagement, and too much waste of our treasure, to be honest with you. I tried and tried to talk Will out of it, but he wouldn't have any of it. He was stubborn, just like I am. He was my best friend, my only sibling, and I didn't want him to go."

Brownlee stopped, closed his eyes, and then continued. "I had no idea what it takes to be a Navy SEAL." He opened his eyes and pointed to Armando. "I don't say this to make him feel good. He doesn't need to hear it from me. He knows what people think of him. I say it to you because it's a confession."

Armando squirmed in his chair. He wanted to be anywhere but in this room right now. His capacity for close emotional connection was lacking. He needed a quick run on the beach, a few dozen pullups, or a midnight swim in the ocean. He didn't need this room, and he certainly didn't need this well-respected doctor to bare his soul. It wasn't anything he wanted to listen to or do himself.

When he looked up at Dr. Brownlee, he felt sorry for the man.

Dr. Brownlee continued on while Armando tried to tune it out.

"And those of us who have lost somebody, whether it's due to an act of war, an accident, illness, cancer, or my brother lost in Grenada, we have to understand they do what they do because they love to do what they do. I resented Will for not coming home, for breaking my parents' hearts. I resented him because he was my best friend. He was my best friend in college. Growing up we did all kinds of crazy things as you can only imagine."

Several people snickered.

"Oh, you too?" one of the men said. "I wasn't a twin, but my younger brother and I used to date the same girls. And we would drive each other crazy with jealousy."

"Yes. Yes to all of that," Dr. Brownlee said. "Maybe I shouldn't say this, but you guys are the lucky ones. Because you get to have the experience of serving in the military or having a loved one who served in the military, and you've also experienced loss. I'm going to reveal something I just discovered. I told Armando just the other day, and I actually thought it was so brilliant I might put it in my next book."

Again, more laughter from the group.

"But I told him it was normal to feel like your love for them, your plans for them, your future with them is unfinished. Very normal. In fact, as I told Armando, nobody ever thinks they have enough time. And we all underestimate how much time we do have."

He examined the room again and then pulled his hands out to the sides. "That's it."

Armando heard sniffles and soft moans. Several

couples hugged themselves, a couple of the men wiped away tears they didn't want anyone to see, and a few sat stoically, mostly looking at the ground and contemplating. But one person didn't do that, and it shocked Armando all the way to his core.

Directly across the room from him sat a young woman that he knew quite well. She wore a purple dress, and her hair was conservatively pulled into a braid and crossed the top of her head just like Armando's mother did every single day. Her eyes and her skin tone were as dark as Armando's. She wore bright orange lipstick and very, very dark eyeliner. Her hair was jet black and shiny.

The woman looked like she'd just risen from the pits of hell itself. She stared at him, and he felt the hatred coursing through her body.

He had never felt that way before in the good old U.S. of A.

CHAPTER 18

S AMBRA STARED BACK at the tall dark man across the room, the man who was responsible for the death of her husband. Her heartbeat elevated even greater than when she first walked in the room and saw him speaking to several others. He hadn't noticed her. And she would've gone the whole length of the meeting without introducing herself or calling attention to him. But now she was caught.

She felt like a bug with the pin stuck through her middle, wiggling in some collector's box—some medieval ritual time warp where she was hooked between life and death, between the passions of love and lost love, and the passions of hate.

Just studying his face, he didn't look like a killer. He didn't look like a man who could snuff out someone's life. And indeed, he didn't shoot her husband in the forehead like that sniper did in Africa. But it was what he did passively, sticking by his wife during a difficult time. She'd hardened herself when she realized they lost the baby anyway, but that still didn't take away the intensity of the hatred she felt for him.

Logically, he wasn't really responsible for Erik's death. Because he was doing the right thing, just like her husband was making the right choice to fill in the spot that Armando vacated. They were all doing the honorable job they were trained for.

But it was absolutely the wrong thing for Sambra.

And now, with the news that her culture and her family had also been stolen by a military man, a government agency, or a couple of well-meaning peaceniks and childless hippie adults from Portland, it didn't matter who did it. She had been damaged. Uprooted and plopped in the middle of a society that she wasn't fated to call her own. Done without her permission, forever altering her life.

And so now she sat in a room, listening to the birds chirping around them. The happy buzz of people greeting each other, eating cookies and sipping coffee in such a civilized manner, covering up and making nice all the terrible things of war and how people held power over other people and victimized them surrounded her. She was participating in the power struggle, of being just one of thousands or perhaps millions of young children who never had a chance to embrace their real family—the family they were intended to have.

She was grateful for her adoptive parents, even though they'd been ill-equipped for a stubborn, strong-minded rebellious youngster, then grade schooler, then young woman, who, unlike her parents, couldn't stand the rigors of high school, and would've run away at ten if she were allowed to. Especially to her father, giving up school was a sacrilege.

In the end, they were the first to give up on her. They let her leave at sixteen years of age, filed the police reports but let her go with some guy—Sambra tried to remember his name and couldn't. He was the flavor of the month, the one who had a car that could drive all the way down the coast to Mexico.

But they got stuck in San Diego. Just like their engine blew up and dashed their lofty plans of living on the beach and eating fish tacos, so too did their relationship. Sambra worked in a variety of odd jobs and tried to go to beauty school, which would have fried her mother who never wore makeup and never shaved a hair on her body.

Nothing worked for her. Now she knew why. It wasn't supposed to work. Her parents had taken away her chances—all of them.

She lived on the beach, paid for her keep with sex, partied away all her money, called home only to let her parents know she was still alive, and grew up without any help from the adults who were never in her life anyway.

Luckily, she didn't get pregnant and eventually realized the dangers of living homeless in a zoo of mental illness and drug addiction. She looked and felt like a throwaway child.

And indeed, she was.

She'd just turned twenty when she met Erik. Strong, handsome Erik with hands that could hold basketballs and yet trembled as he touched her the first time. He'd been a virgin, which she quickly remedied, and then became her rabid student.

Sex was sacred to Erik. She was grateful for that gift because she'd never experienced that. She missed how he cherished her. She missed his kisses, she missed how hard he worked to come home early, to show her that he loved her by bringing her flowers. No one in her life had ever done this. And just as she was beginning to believe this could actually be, this man in front of her decided to stay home, and Erik sacrificed his life in his place.

She told this dark man across the room that he should have died in Erik's place. She told him that mentally, and for just a second, Sambra thought he got it.

She was forced to look away and quickly wiped a tear from her right eye.

People were milling around, crossing and stopping in the middle of the room, many of them forming a small circle around Armando. They were welcoming him, greeting him. He was part of their tribe. He was, after all, a revered Navy SEAL. She could see in the faces of some of the men that they didn't feel worthy. Yet they were, every single one of them were. There was nothing special about this man. Just like there was nothing special about Erik, except for how he was wired. How he didn't quit, how he lived large. He had planned to make that slice of the American Dream way bigger than he was dealt, and that was one of the many reasons she loved him with abandon.

Another tear formed in the corner of her eye. She just let it spill over the edge and drip onto her hands clasped in her lap. She was shaking.

A shadow crossed her body, and when she looked up, it was the kind face of Dr. Brownlee. "Are you alright? If you need to, you can go outside and get a little air."

She understood now why people loved him, why this man was so famous, why his book had sold millions of copies. How he was an expert on military suicides and grief counseling. He had the capacity to be more than the sum of the parts he was given. In that respect, he was just like Erik, who was raised on a poor rural farm, parents scraping to get by, but so proud of their son when he got his Trident. They wouldn't give up, either, even though their phone calls were less frequent and she'd asked them to stop sending the afghans and embroidered pillow cases that only made her weep for hours at a time.

"I'm sorry, Doctor. I just got overwhelmed. I'm— I'm hoping I don't have to leave."

"Leave whenever you like. No one is forcing you to stay. You do what's right for you. Don't worry about the rest of us. And don't be sorry, Sambra. This is what we do here. We expose our feelings."

"But I don't want to. They're mine. They belong to me and me alone."

"You think so? Do you think there's anything you could say that someone else in this room hasn't had something similar happen or thought? We are all much more alike than we are separate. We are one family. And this group in particular is a brotherhood that will live forever, even though some of the families have gone on."

His kind blue eyes felt like a refreshing waterfall over her skin. He extended his hands out in front, which could have turned into a hug, if she let him. But instead, she stood bracing herself with one hand in each of his. Closer to his face, she could see in his eyes he too carried the scars of grief and despair. She was surprised at this.

"So, Doctor, death takes from all of us, is that right?" She turned her chin to the side, scanning Armando and the group of people around him. Just then, the SEAL glanced back at her. And there was an electric connection there, but again, she looked away.

She knew Brownlee saw it, but he didn't let on. "Well said, my dear."

My dear is what he said. Just like Assad. Just like Ansari, just like the men who said they could put her back in touch with her village, her people, her bloodline, her family. This man was telling her she was already part of the tribe of military families—of those that have lost loved ones after having served. And how lucky for Sambra that her husband died a hero and not a casualty of suicide. There was a mother here who was facing that still, after ten years of trying to put it behind her.

"I will stay, as long as I feel I'm contributing. But I really don't want to sit here as a crying blubbering basket case of a woman. Because that's not who I am," she said defiantly.

"Sambra, I have no doubt that is one hundred percent accurate. And I can't wait until you find that again. Because when you do, you will light up the room."

She liked that thought.

"How do you know I won't blow it up?" she said, in

a husky and mysterious voice.

Dropping hands, she left the doctor and looked for the mother who had been recounting the days after her son's suicide. She found her in the corner with a Kleenex, holding hands with another young woman. And then, as she got closer, she could see that they were sharing some happy moment or some prank because her tears were tears of joy. Both of them laughing, both of them enjoying the share between them, the island of healing between them in a murky dark sea of despair.

"I was sitting over there and thinking how I didn't know who to talk to or what to say. I was crying, and I saw you, and here I thought you were having a melt-down. I came over to help."

Instead of quietly nodding, the woman laughed. She actually laughed!

Penny, the young woman who had joined her, wiped tears from her eyes with the backs of her hand. "You're Sambra, right?"

"Yes." Sambra was still confused, though.

Penny began to give her an explanation, "She and I were talking about care packages she used to send her son overseas. I used to send them to my husband as well. I lost him four years ago now. He was in the Army Special Forces, and well, one time I sent him the wrong package. I had bought a gift for my sister, and then I had bought him a really crazy looking t-shirt. He loved t-shirts. He used to wear them even though sometimes he got in trouble for doing so under his uniform. I always got white ones, so they wouldn't see. So I sent my sister the t-shirt, and I sent my husband a pink negligee."

The older woman laughed again. "Oh, that is the best story I've ever heard. My son actually didn't mind the scented toilet paper I sent him. They had quite a good time with it in the barracks, I guess. It was supposed to come to me, and I forgot to change the address on the postage so it went to the last previous mailing that I'd done, and I'd sent him some brownies that—" She looked at both Sambra and then Penny. "Well, the brownies never got there, but he did get the scented toilet paper, and the whole platoon had a good laugh over it."

The woman's angelic face stared down at her hands and her toes painted with red nail polish, Sambra's favorite, popping through her flip flops.

Normal, Sambra thought. This is all normal. *I didn't want to be normal. I never wanted to be normal. I just wanted to be loved.*

She sighed. "I miss him."

Neither of the two ladies responded except Penny curled her arm around her shoulder. "Yes, sweetheart. We all do."

THE REST OF the meeting was like sitting in a small rowboat on a choppy sea. Some of the shares were very rich and poignant, some were difficult to hear, and some people were so bottled up with whatever demons they were battling they could hardly express themselves. But everyone did eventually open up. One by one, the group took turns looking at Sambra. She had attended the meeting three days before but had said nothing. And she was intending to do the same today.

Brownlee pretended that he didn't notice, but Sambra knew he did. Armando couldn't take his eyes off her. It was as if he was calling out that bitterness and rancor she felt toward him. Like he was daring her to show it in front of the whole group. So she decided to give it a whirl and ruin everyone's morning. At least that's what she thought she'd do.

"Well, I can see by the way you're all looking at me that it's my turn. And I wasn't going to say anything because I don't think I have much to offer." She glanced around the room, her eyes lighting on Armando. He was holding his breath.

She sat up straight, uncrossing her legs and crossing them the other direction, and scratched the back of her head. Then, with her forefinger, twirled her wayward strands of hair at the back of her neck.

"I may not be the most recent victim of the death of a family member, in this case my husband. But I am still seething with hatred and rage." She purposely stared at the ground.

"I knew Erik for about two months before we got married. I met him in a bar; we got drunk together. We spent the night screwing our brains out. And the next morning, I fell in love with him. I mean, I fell in love with everything about him. He was kind. He was handsome, tall, and physically fit. He was a man, not a boy, not like the boys I'd been dating. I basically came to San Diego to run away from all kinds of things, and I lived here for some time trying to get odd jobs here and there. I lived in places you wouldn't want to know about. Sometimes I slept on the beach. So we were just partying at a bar with a couple of the girls from the temp agency I worked for. And there he was. He was with several of his buddies. Eating french fries. Who knew he would become my husband?"

She looked up and scanned the room. Her comments were having the effect on the group that she expected. Some were pensive; some fidgeted, making the chairs squeak; some shook their heads slightly. A few outright frowns came her way, and a couple people gave her a friendly smile, but she knew there was much more behind those smiles. She wasn't making marks for popularity, but then again, that wasn't what she was here for. She was here to tell him how she felt. That's what Dr. Brownlee said was her job. And she was going to be good at her job.

"We were married about a year and five to six months. During that time, he passed the rest of his courses to become a Navy SEAL. And he was ready for his first deployment, waiting for a chance to be positioned. He was trained as a marksman, a sharpshooter, and he was deadly accurate in all ranges with all weapons. My handsome, big, stubborn, beautiful, strong husband was a killer. But as it turns out, he got an opportunity that had been passed up by someone else. And he took that SEAL's place."

She stared at Armando who lifted his chin, accepted her perusal, and stuck his chest out. She could see his lower lip quiver ever so slightly.

"Imagine my shock when I found out my husband was shot dead in the forehead on his very first deployment. And the man whose place he took, today, on this beautiful San Diego morning, is sitting in this very room with me."

A hush fell upon the group, one of those combined sighs Sambra used to hear in a movie theater or at a football game or from a distance in a park where people were playing volleyball.

She had fractured the day.

CHAPTER 19

A RMANDO WAS GOING to scramble to his feet and leave the room. He'd had just about all he could take from this woman, who seemed hell-bent on bringing her own private version of torture and dumping it in the middle of the floor. The room was abuzz with objections. People scowled and whispered to each other, shaking their heads and generally erupting into cross talk and counter-cross talk; it was pure bedlam. So Armando might have been able to slip out without anyone noticing, except that Dr. Brownlee did.

The doctor's hand raised in a stop motion, first to Armando and then the group. As he stood to calm people, he let them all know everyone who wanted to would get a chance to share, but that it was imperative the people not interrupt or yell over each other.

"I'm going to stop you now, because this is quite explosive." He turned to Sambra. "I understand your pain, and I understand—and forgive me, I didn't think—I understand that it probably wasn't a good idea for you to be in this group with this gentleman. And that's on me. So if you're going to blame somebody about this situation today, you can blame me all you want. And I will still tell you this is in no way who you are. This is something you are going to regret. I don't say this to you in a form of a reprimand, but it's just a fact."

Armando noted that Sambra remained seated, nodded her head, crossed her arms and legs, and stared back down at the floor.

"Now as far as the rest of you, some of you probably reacted rather strongly to her comments."

There were shouts of agreement and some unkind swearing. Someone even shouted over the din that Sambra should leave immediately.

"Let's take a minute and breathe. Just like Sambra's behavior is possibly understandable, and she's going to have to explain to you if she intended to cause you harm or not, some of you have something very strong to say to her. So let me just caution you. I can say this to this group of people because you are familiar with the ebb and flow of life, the fog of war, the confusion, the pain, and the horror of it. Most wars are started from comments, did you know that?"

The crowd wasn't having any of it and still wanted

to get unruly.

"You could say that people send their sons and daughters off to fight, because someone else in another part of the world has picked a fight. Then your families are required to pay the price. It's a very unfair assumption, and it's extremely crude. I apologize for that. But when you think of your comments, I want you to be truthful and honest, but don't vent your anger here. We can do that in private sessions. Grief can twist the mind, cause reactions you would not otherwise have. Think about that. Think about that in your own life."

Calm was descending over the room. Several attendees who had been standing, ready to leave, sat back down.

"I have just admonished her for doing that. And now I must caution you to not do the same. Keep it between the lines. And this is very useful, even though you may think, 'Oh, what a terrible thing she said, what a terrible person she is. She doesn't belong here.' You and I both know that in the days and weeks and years to come, and for some it's already happened several times, something will set you off. Something's going to get your ego out of whack, and you're going to respond negatively. Someone's going to say something that you deep down in your core don't understand how they could be so cruel. I'm not asking you to take it or to like it. I'm asking you to understand. I'm asking you if you can—and I know some of you in this group have shown great capacity for it—if you can show compassion. But tell her the truth. Tell her how she made you feel. She needs to hear it." He turned, sat back down in his seat, and added, "I'm done."

The first person Dr. Brownlee looked at was Armando.

One by one, several in the group explained how they'd had similar feelings toward certain people after the death of their loved ones. There were many who found fault with all sorts of people, including themselves. Some felt guilty they had had an argument with the person who never came home afterwards. Or that they'd said something unkind they didn't mean or that they didn't tell them they loved them enough. They regretted their behavior and wished they could do it over.

Armando thought she was treated very kindly. It was not at all on the same level she delivered it. So he felt it was on him to clear it up. To take that big step. She needed to hear the truth, at least his truth.

"Well, since I'm the person who you feel murdered your husband—and I get that you think it was murder—I'm here to tell you that I probably would have wished it was me. I stayed home to take care of my wife, who was pregnant and having complications. We lost the baby, and then I lost her."

Several of the women began to openly cry.

"There was a time, Sambra, when I thought a bullet to my brain would be the right thing to do. Because I felt so guilty for Erik's death. And he was a kid I trained. I taught him all the best things I'd learned over the years about marksmanship. He'd been a hunter his whole life, but I taught him how to think tactically, how to get into places where he would be hidden so he could protect his team. He was an avid student, eager to show his chops. If I had gone in place of him at the last minute, he would've been so pissed off at me, Sambra. He would've practically knocked my lights out. What I'm saying is that he *wanted* to go."

Several people chuckled.

"I spent a couple of weeks—well, no, not that long. About eight days I think—getting drunk as a skunk. I considered going to strip clubs, thought about all the different ways I could end my life without bringing suffering and pain to my family, the family I still had. And if it weren't for my little three-year-old son, Artemis, the spitting image of my wife, Gina, I might have. I really might have."

There was dead silence in the room.

"I don't recommend it, by the way. I'm not saying that here."

Several chuckled.

"I don't know if you remember what Dr. Brownlee

said when he started this meeting, but he talked about how we never have enough time. And finally at the end of my drunken stupors, I realized, that I had a life left. I had the responsibility to Artemis, to my elderly mother, to my sometimes wayward and feisty sister, and my brother-in-law who always tries to be the recipient of her passion but not the recipient of her anger."

Again, more chuckles.

"I want to watch Artemis learn to ride a bike. I'd like to teach him to shoot squirrels, not cats or dogs, but squirrels. Maybe rabbits. I want to teach him how to gut a fish with a knife or dress a deer. I want to teach him how to ride a roller coaster without puking."

Several in the group were having a difficult time containing themselves.

"I don't mean to be funny, and I don't mean to be casual to your situation, because I have a tremendous amount of respect for women, especially who are left behind when the love of their life exits stage left. I lost my own father when I was a boy. I know the toll it took on my mother, and it facilitated our coming to San Diego from Puerto Rico. I'm the son of immigrants.

"What I decided to do was to learn how to be in control. So I took my anger and my pain, and I turned it into action. When I was sitting there on the couch with my booze, I thought to myself, this is not the man I am. This isn't the boy who survived his father's death.

This isn't the boy who promised his mother he would take care of her forever. This is not the man who would abandon his child without his child ever getting to know him or hear stories about his mother. And that's when I decided to try, just try to forgive. Try to put it behind me."

Sambra's face was lined with tears, but she would not look away. Just like she'd said, she didn't quit. And she didn't quit on Armando just now. She took the words, she took them to heart, and she'd let her eyes show the whole group the pain of her insides.

That took courage.

Maybe it wasn't enough for her, but it filled him with joy.

CHAPTER 20

S AMBRA LEFT THE meeting room as soon as it was over. She didn't wait to see if anyone wanted to speak to her, she just wanted to get as far away from these people as she could.

Driving down the strand, she passed surf shops, dress stores, fancy jewelry stores—all places where she and Erik had walked, dreamed, and window-shopped.

Everything was a blur.

Of course, that was partly because she could hardly see through her tears, and as she went through several intersections and then turned toward the expressway taking her back to her place, the emotions inside just started to pour out, and her whole upper body shook. At a stop light, she placed her forehead against the steering wheel and sobbed.

Honking behind her told her that the light had changed. She gunned it and took off on the expressway.

She thought she knew what she was doing, how she was thinking. She'd hoped working with the immigration attorney would help her to find some kind of focus. At first, the anger and hatred she was consumed with seemed to make her stronger, almost like a tough workout or an endurance run. She thought cutting herself off from anything respectable, honorable, or normal about anybody in that community, specifically the SEAL community, was a good thing. She had been done with it, or so she thought.

As she continued to struggle with her breathing, her head was filled with memories of things she didn't want to think about between sobs. She envisioned her father with his scraggly, sandy gray ponytail and metal rimmed spectacles pouring over a book he was going to be discussing at his college-level English class. She saw her mother making some herbal remedy for a bee sting or something that had befallen Sambra. This second look at them wasn't the horrific scene she had been telling herself.

She'd heard the stories, how her parents thought they were doing the right thing by adopting her. Her mother told her once she thought that perhaps it would fill the void of their childless marriage. But they discovered that wasn't the case. And that wasn't Sambra's fault, either.

They didn't abandon her, she suddenly realized.

They didn't have the capacity to feel or to love to the same depth and degree that she did, to give what she apparently needed. And so, while other children pondered whether or not they were adopted because they didn't seem to have much in common with their parents, Sambra had embraced that theory, because she knew she didn't come from her parents. She came from somewhere else.

She began to understand they perhaps did the best they could do. And that wasn't good enough for her. That didn't make her wrong or some kind of a freakish princess who had to have it all her own way. It's just that she needed something more, just like they did.

She felt the guilt for having so angrily reacted. Armando didn't deserve what she was dishing out, either. He had actually shown her he had weathered a storm much worse than hers.

And despite facing that nightmare, he'd found a way. He embraced something new that was positive. He found something to live for.

That's what she needed.

After a half hour of driving, she realized she'd gone way past her turnoff. Where was she? Why had she come here? All of a sudden, she didn't recognize the neighborhood. She didn't recognize the houses or the addresses or the stores. It was a district, a very ethnic district filled with all sorts of nationalities and eateries, vibrant and alive, ready for evening action. It was also a tourist destination for some. She'd never been here before. She decided to park in the streets and find a restaurant. Perhaps some food might help her calm her nerves. She located a Mexican deli and ordered black beans, rice, and a chile relleno. She also ordered a beer.

The food was delicious, people spoke in different languages in the restaurant, and music blared. The place was literally jumping with activity. Why was it that she felt she couldn't have an American experience in an American city with American parents when the cultural diversity was all around her? Why did she have to feel that her culture had been hidden from her?

There were only two things her parents ever disagreed with. One was when she dropped out of school. Her father tried to get her back in, urging her to try again by switching schools, teachers, or getting tutoring, but to no avail.

How did she pay them back? She ran away.

Then came the news she was going to marry a Navy SEAL. Even that they accepted, although both her parents had heavy ties to the anti-war community and had been arrested many times for protests. They had protested every skirmish and outbreak the Americans were ever involved in. Her father'd chained himself to fences, attended riotous meetings, and boycotted large corporations who didn't share his values. He was a zealot, on the opposite side as her husband.

What was she thinking? How else would they react? Why did she expect so much of them?

The meeting with her parents had gone poorly. Erik was labeled a trained killer. She thought her poor husband-to-be was going to pull her father out of the house by his ponytail.

Erik fought for her. Insisted he loved her. "I swear to you I will never allow anything to ever hurt her. If you try to separate us, I'll hunt you down and make you pay for your mistake."

No one had fought like that for her. She remembered how good it felt to have someone come to her defense.

Her parents didn't come to the wedding, but they accepted the marriage. And when he was killed, they kept their distance. Sambra felt the bond between them was finally severed. She was truly on her own. Sambra was done.

Now, she had a chance with a new family, perhaps her real family. She decided to give Assad Nefrusia a call.

She didn't expect he'd still be in the office, but he picked up on the first ring.

"How very nice to hear from you, Sambra. Listen, we have much to talk about. Khalil has located a cousin. We aren't quite sure how distant he is, but he said it was a cousin he met once in Paris. And he's traveled here. His cousin would like to meet you."

"Okay. I'm going to be heading home soon. When?"

"Tomorrow? Are you available in the morning? Could you meet us at my home? Less formal that way."

"Sure. Will Khalil be there too?"

"He is temporarily with us until his Fall semester starts. It's a special favor to the boy and to Ansari. I have plenty of room."

"Fine. What time were you thinking?"

"Nine?"

"I'll be there." She paused and then added, "I-I just wanted to say something to clear the air, Mr. Nefrusia. You mentioned something about immigration issues, and other family members. And Ansari said something about another brother of mine. Khalil says that there was a brother of mine who passed away after they moved to Paris. Do you know what happened to him? Is there another brother that I'm waiting for, or, other than this cousin, is Khalil all the family that you've located?"

"We have located several people that remember your parents or lived in the same village as your family, and some of them indeed might be your blood relatives. What you have to understand is everyone was scattered all over Europe and the United States. Some even immigrated to South America."

"To South America? Syrians in South America?"

"There are lots of people moving all the time, my dear. And after conflicts like this, they scatter and put down roots wherever they can. Not every country will take them in. So you can have family members in Europe and family members in, say, Chile or Columbia or Venezuela. You can have family members in Canada or Hong Kong."

"I wasn't aware of that."

"This is why the work I'm doing is so important. We are really trying to bring people back together who were separated. We want to recreate the family that was torn apart by the skirmishes. And it is a calling for which I am extremely proud. I think you are very lucky to have such a fine brother and his network of friends. He's a very smart boy, and I expect big things from him in the future. You as well, Sambra."

"It's all confusing, I admit. But I really want to meet my family. Will this cousin have any details, do you think?"

"I am hoping so. If not now, we will continue to dig. If we all work together, you'll be united with your people. You'll see. And don't worry about being confused. There's a lot to take in. This is your opportunity to broaden your horizons, to learn how to be a world citizen. And none of this would be possible without the work of our organization. So consider yourself lucky, and we'll look forward to seeing you two tomorrow."

Sambra was excited for the new adventure. Calling him was definitely the right choice. It brightened her spirits and brought so many other things into focus.

After Assad hung up, she paid her luncheon bill and made it home just before dark. She stripped down and took a long hot shower, washing her hair, dreaming about travel, foreign lands, and a loving family around her. She was drying her hair when she heard her phone ring.

"Sambra? This is Armando. Armando Guzman. Please don't hang up."

"I'm not going to hang up on you, Armando. But I'm still processing what went on today. Not exactly sure what I have to say to you."

"I understand. I want to propose something. Like a truce. Would you join me tomorrow for coffee, if you're available? My mother's going to take my son to a little event at his preschool, and I have a couple of free hours. I thought maybe we could just sit and maybe learn a little bit about each other. I am not trying to push at all, and this isn't going to be a conversation where I'm schooling you or getting angry at you for some of the deep-seated feelings that you have. I understand them, to the contrary."

"I'm still not sure it's a good idea. I like the idea of the group setting. I like the idea of ground rules and Dr. Brownlee being there to sort of monitor things."

"Very well."

She could tell he was hedging about something.

"You sound disappointed. Is everything okay?" she asked.

"I'm not sure I'm going to be attending the group any longer. But I would like the opportunity to just talk. Not accuse or yell or ask for forgiveness or blame. I just want to understand you. And I want to give you the opportunity, if you're willing, to understand me. I have some very fond memories of Erik. He was one of my best—one of my special students. And you know I feel bad about what happened. Would you do me that favor? It's just coffee."

"I've agreed to meet an immigration attorney in Los Angeles tomorrow morning. I suppose I could postpone it to the afternoon, but I'll have to see if he'd be agreeable to doing it later."

"I can't do the afternoon. I have a group I'm supposed to take out to the island for target practice. And that one the Navy won't let me reschedule. But I am available until noon. If you'll listen to what I have to say."

"Okay. I will let them know, and I guess I can text you back at this number if it's not a go?"

"Yes. Until tomorrow then. And, Sambra, thank you."

He disconnected the call before she could respond. Now she was going to have two adventures tomorrow. Neither one of them were anything like the other. But they both filled her with excitement.

Lying in bed, she whispered to herself, "Maybe I can do this. Maybe, Erik, if you'll help me, maybe I can do this. I still love you. But I'm going to need your help."

CHAPTER 21

ARMANDO WAITED AT the Cafe Amici Coffee Shop just off the Strand. He had dropped Artemis off with Gus and Felicia and was early for the 9:00 meeting he'd set up with Sambra.

He had given their group session yesterday with Dr. Brownlee a lot of thought, and he wasn't happy with everything he said, but he agreed that cracking the eggshell of this negativity between the two of them was a good thing. He had no interest in being a big part of Sambra's life. He just didn't believe she should harbor as much resentment as she did. And he thought perhaps he could fix that.

"You're always fixing things, Armani. Let it go," Kyle had said when he told him last night.

T.J. stared at him across the picnic table at The Scupper and then, after he'd gotten his fill, said his piece. "I'm trying to figure out, for the life of me, why you want to do this? I mean, I've not seen you do this for anybody else, and I think it's pretty clear she doesn't want much to do with you. Don't you think you'd be sort of making things worse?"

Armando thought he made a good point, but he wasn't ready to give up.

"I guess I'm thinking, what would Erik want us to do? Would he want her to just remove herself from the community while hating the Navy, hating me or anybody on the team? I mean, personally, I can stand it if that's the way she wants to leave it. But is that really what our brother would want? Aren't we charged with taking care of her, somehow?"

Kyle's chin had touched his chest as he looked up at the group through his eyelashes. His mouth was downturned in a frown. "Oh boy. Here we go. We got drama, drama, drama, and more drama." He turned his face to look Armani straight in the eyes. "You sure you want to do this? I mean, what's in it for you? What if you do make it worse? You want that on your conscience?"

"Well, I think she's pretty well out the door, and I don't see how we could do worse. I mean, I'm not going to be angry with her. Even if she gets upset with me, I'm not going to be angry with her. I just, I want her to understand that this is really what her husband wanted. If something had happened to me and Gina was all blaming you, Kyle, for sending me on a mission

I shouldn't have gone on... I mean, you know this could happen."

"Already has. I've been blamed lots of times. Hell, I got accused by a twelve-year-old girl of sending her father out to get his leg shot off."

"See, that's what I mean—you would do the same if it were Gina, right?"

"Yep." That was all Cooper had to say about the subject.

"But she's not Gina, Armani," said T.J.

Fredo had a comment next. "You know, Armani. This kind of reminds me of when you first met Gina. I mean, remember you were having all that trouble with Mia, and she was, I mean, she was driving you nuts."

Everybody laughed at that one. Cooper pointed a finger at Fredo. "Mia was driving *you* nuts. She was teasing your ass all over the place, and you were sitting right here just like what Armando's doing and saying that you thought you could help her."

The group chuckled again at Fredo's expense.

Fredo threw his napkin at Coop. "I rest my case. It is the same. These women somehow think that. They just go crazy. I mean, Mia knew she was doing things that weren't good for her, they weren't good for her child, and, Armani, you couldn't stop her from being so self-destructive. You tried, didn't you?"

"That I did. That's a fact."

"And you thought Gina was just like Mia. You thought she was someone who liked to get into trouble, but you learned that she wasn't. She was a good girl. She was a cop. You guys helped her catch the bad guy, and in the process, well..." Fredo showed his palms to the group. "Like I said, I rest my case."

Now, sitting at the little table in the coffee shop, he reconsidered his choice of venue. He had thought it would be noisy enough to mask any kind of discussion that Sambra might think would be too personal. It turned out that today, of all days, nobody was there. He got up and ordered a second cappuccino, reminding himself that if he got too jittery, he wouldn't be able to think straight. He considered having them put a shot of liquor in his coffee cup, but remembered his promise to Dr. Brownlee that he was going to swear off alcohol for thirty days.

"Sucks. Why did I make that pledge?" he asked under his breath.

Sambra had parked her car across the street and was waiting for the opportunity to cross when she looked up and noticed him in the window. She had beautiful black hair she wore long today. He had never seen her style it that way. Her slim hips and long legs made an attractive picture crossing the road, and she had no trouble getting cars to stop for her.

Inside the shop, she closed the door behind her,

which tinkled the bell at the top, ignored him, and instead greeted the barista behind the counter. The two of them spoke for several minutes while the machine squealed, and then Sambra brought a cappuccino over to the table and joined him.

"Sorry, I know her. We worked together for a while."

Armando shook his head. "No problem. You want to buy your own coffee? You go right ahead. But the next one's on me."

He sat back in his chair and waited until she got settled, took her first sip, and then leaned into the grainy marble top. Today, her eyes appeared even darker than before. Her black hair was cascading in wiry ringlets all over her head and shoulders. She brushed curly bangs from her forehead and took another sip.

"So what did you want to talk to me about?"

He was fixated on her red-orange nail polish. He had thought she wore Gina's favorite color, but upon examining it closer, he noticed it was more orange than red.

"I guess I came to see if we could find some common ground here. I don't wish you any harm. And I really want you to understand that, although the outbursts seem to get a big reaction out of the group, I don't exactly feel the same way about it. I just, I think that you need to be told the truth about certain things. When I've had to go through something challenging, I've always appreciated it when somebody was direct. When somebody didn't try to pussyfoot around and told me straight."

"I'm the same way. I'm probably more impulsive, but—"

"You think?"

She gave him a smirk. "I suppose I deserve that. I've been called a princess before." And then something inside her began to crumble, because that was her husband's favorite word for her. *Princess*.

He gave a slight nod. "I have a lot of respect for Erik. He was a good kid. I have to tell you, he was just head over heels about being married to you. He told me every chance he could how nice, how beautiful, how fantastic you were and how lucky he felt."

Armando stared down at his coffee and stirred it with the miniature spoon. "You should know that. You should know that he wasn't afraid. You should know he actually tried to get on Kyle's team for months. He was going to be assigned to SEAL Team 5. You may not have been told the story."

"No. He never told me any of that. I know he liked to hunt and shoot. He didn't want to be placed on a team where he was going to be used for something else."

"Exactly. That's what we do. We put good people with different talents on the teams, and we call them up as we need them. We do that all the time."

Armando struggled as he searched the traffic moving back and forth on the busy street.

"I guess I don't really know what I want to say to you. I just, if I could just give you some advice, if I could do anything, I just want to tell you how much you were loved. And if he were here today, Sambra, he would tell you that. I feel like I'm his brother in this crazy brotherhood of men. As his brother, I should be his voice right now and make sure that you get it, that you really get it. Because yesterday in the group, it was like you were telling me the love in your life is gone. But that's not true. It's still there. He still loves you from wherever he is, and you will always love him. You know that, right?"

Sambra examined her fingernails and her empty coffee cup.

"You want another?" he asked.

"I'm good." She continued to stare at the foam collecting at the bottom of the ceramic. "It sounds like you're telling me walking away from this brotherhood, as you call it, is walking away from him as well."

"Yes! That's exactly what I'm saying. Look, I'm always going to love Gina. She will always be my true love, my wife, my son's mother. But someday, if I'm lucky and if I want it to happen, I will find somebody else. Or not. And it really doesn't matter if it does or doesn't happen. But Gina will always be with me. There isn't anything that will take her away. And I love Artemis, but the love of Artemis doesn't interfere with the love I have for his mother. That's how love works. It expands. We don't get well by closing it off or thinking to ourselves that it's never coming back. There's always a chance, always."

He saw he hit a nerve with her. Her eyes began to tear up, her lips in a tight smirk as if she was thinking of something tough and didn't want to say it.

"Go ahead. You can tell me anything you want. I meant that. I can take it," he said and waited.

She inhaled a deep breath, sat straight in her chair, and then leaned forward with her elbows on the cool stone top. "Those were the exact words that your Gina told me." She smiled. "She told me that I would find love again. How interesting. When I heard that advice coming from her, I wondered where it was coming from. And now I can see it was the way your relationship was. I never got to get to know my Erik that well."

Armando reached across the table and patted her arm. "I'm going to stop you there. Because it doesn't matter. I knew from the very first time I met Gina that she was going to be my wife. I was conflicted because of the circumstances under which we met, but I knew that somehow she was going to be part of my future."

"This is really bizarre, Armando, because we talked about this, but not with these results. How could she have known she was not going to be here for you, for Artemis, for me. I told her that we were all bound together, the four of us, that it was some kind of a plan, some kind of a coincidence that wasn't a coincidence at all, that somebody upstairs had destined this would happen."

Her face got pink, and she diverted her eyes. Armando didn't want to pry further, sensing she felt she'd overstepped somehow. He pulled his hand away and set it in his lap.

"Well, you just think about that then. Think about a future that you could have. Think about what it would look like, to fall in love."

"And is that what you'll be doing, too?"

It was the first time Armando experienced some kind of warmth coming from this strange woman, as if somebody had changed the red light. And it went from red to yellow.

He wondered what it would be like if it ever turned green.

CHAPTER 22

S AMBRA'S MEETING WITH Armando had buoyed her
spirits. For the first time in weeks, she actually
looked forward to interesting days ahead. She felt the
love of her countrymen, new family, and her local
friends, as well as support coming from her husband's
side, the SEAL Community, keeping his memory alive.
After all, that is where she wanted to come down. She
wanted to maintain the memory—the good memory—
of her marriage to Erik.

There had been an unusual light rain that had
started just as she left the coffee shop, washing the
streets, giving everything a fresh makeover. She loved
how the rains in San Diego brought the colors out;
hence, the flavors and smells of the ocean, the restaurants, the rib bars and the coffee shops along the strand
permeated the air. People seemed happier after a rain,
probably because it didn't happen as often as it did up
in Oregon or Northern California.

She parked her car, waved to a couple of busboys who were smoking cigarettes outside the deli-restaurant, and skipped down the narrow alleyway to the corner. Turning, she took the steps to the second floor of Assad's residence two steps at a time. She had more energy, was excited, and loved the feeling of being alive.

Khalil answered the door when she knocked. He opened it wide and gave her a broad smile. "Sister!"

Before he could step back and allow her entry, she grabbed him around the shoulders and gave him a huge hug, which nearly toppled the both of them. At his displeasure, and due to the fact that he turned bright red and stared at the ground, she giggled.

She noted Ansari's head peep around the kitchen doorway. His bright smile indicated his pleasure. "I'm so glad to see you two get along so well. It just warms my heart."

Sambra entered the center of the living room, set down her purse, and, with her hands placed together, asked the question to both men, "So where are they? Where are our cousins?"

Ansari was, as usual, impeccably dressed. With his well-groomed and buffed nails, he extended his hand. "Sambra, my dear, you are so beautiful. You light up this whole room. I am enchanted," he placed his other hand over his chest, "every time I get to see you again."

She stepped back. "But where are they? You're not answering my question." She feigned a mock disapproval, playing with him.

Khalil merely stood and watched the banter between the two of them, expressionless.

Ansari cleared his throat and said, "He has gone to the bus depot to pick up your cousins. Isn't that right, Khalil?" he asked her brother.

"Yes, yes. He left about an hour ago. He said he would be back soon."

"So, Khalil, when do I get to meet Assad's family? I've met his missus, but I have never met his children."

Khalil looked up at Ansari. The handsome gentleman responded with another bright smile.

"They are away at school. Assad's two youngest children are going to be taking a trip with their mother very soon. I think today, they are preparing for this trip. I'm sure in time you will get to meet them and hopefully before they leave."

She was satisfied for the moment but found herself eager now that she'd agreed to become part of their community and meet part of her generic family. She was embracing the opportunity to meet everyone she could, starving for information.

"You would like some coffee, my dear?"

The way Ansari always said *my dear* was pleasing, as if he too were an older brother of hers, an uncle, or someone very familiar with her family. He was in an exceptionally good mood today, with his eyes sparkling, his smiles generous, and his movements gracious and catlike. He held a chair for her to sit and asked again, "Coffee?"

Sambra was aware that part of her excitement was due to all the caffeine she'd had this morning and the stimulating conversation.

"Water please." Then she added, "I've had two or three cappuccinos this morning with a friend. I think if I have any more I'll be peeing all night."

Khalil bowed his head again but showed her a timid smile. Ansari was focused in a different direction.

"Ah, so you are making new friends? Or are you reestablishing your old friendships now?"

"I wouldn't exactly call him a friend—"

"Him?" Ansari asked. "A new boyfriend perhaps?" His eyes danced in flirtatious rhythm with the fluttering of his eyelids. It was almost feminine the way he looked at her.

"Oh, God no. I would not consider him a friend, at least not yet. I know him from our grief counseling group. But beyond that, he was a former teammate of my husband's. And I'm learning to accept the fact he probably was the one responsible for my husband being on the mission. You see he was supposed to go, and he stayed home to take care of his wife."

Ansari nodded his head, brought in a glass of water, and then sat across from her on the table. His brow furrowed ever so slightly. "So you had coffee this morning with a married man?" He was extremely displeased, she could see.

"Oh no. His wife passed much more recently. That's why he's in the group. It was just coincidence he also happened to be an acquaintance of my husband, who helped train him."

"So he is a Navy SEAL instructor, is that correct?"

"No, he *is* a Navy SEAL. But he was senior to my husband with weaponry."

"You wish to be connected with him, the man who is responsible for your husband's untimely death?"

"Not exactly. It's a healing process."

"By communicating with your enemy?"

Sambra was taken aback with his reaction. "I used to feel the same way, Ansari. First, he's not my enemy. And second, I am growing to understand that I can have many families. Not just one. I think losing that one family, my husband, when I had really not established any other is what has made things so difficult."

"But now," he said as he pointed to Khalil. "Now you have new family, people who are of your lineage to you, who care about you, and who share your bloodline."

"I think my husband would feel the same about his

SEAL team. They are in every way brothers to him, just as Khalil and I are brothers. You understand that men who go to war against a common enemy become brothers, correct?"

That seemed to strike home with Ansari. "I understand now, Sambra. Thank you for explaining it to me. It makes perfect sense."

His lips smiled, but his eyes did not.

Several minutes later, Assad and two younger men entered the doorway, carrying packages from the downstairs deli. Sambra stood and prepared to be introduced.

Assad Nefrusia began. "Sambra, these are, I believe, your cousins Viktor and Samir. They have come a long way to meet you."

One by one, she shook their hands. Both men were slightly older than her brother, taller, and seemed to have been westernized, wearing skinny jeans, tee shirts, and sockless loafers. She was grateful there would not be the awkward communication she felt she had with Khalil.

"It's a pleasure to meet you. I have so many questions. And what side of the family are you on?"

Assad jumped in, laughing. "Sambra is so anxious to get to know everybody who knew her family or is part of her family. She is like a sponge, soaking up all the culture and history of her people. And there is so much to talk about and show you. We're thrilled, my dear, to be able to bring you some great news. We think you're going to walk away from here on a cloud." Assad was beaming and then realized he was still holding hot food in bags that were going to rip.

"Oh, I must put this down. Come boys, come. Let's get the meal prepared, and then we shall talk." Before he turned into the kitchen, he stopped to look at her. Samir ran into him, nearly causing him to drop the brown paper bag. "We have pictures, Sambra. Pictures of your family."

The next two hours went by quickly. There were copies of documents and photographs, photographs of a family she never knew or may have met as a baby. She saw pictures of her mother and her father and several other nieces and nephews, as well as pictures of a home before the shelling and the war. She wasn't able to absorb all of it. The names and faces all started to blend together until her brain hurt. But gradually, the story of her family was revealed.

They explained to her that her family had once been in business running a small market, and other relatives of the family raised livestock and horses. They had some relatives who were involved in politics and others who were teachers. She had a great aunt who was a famous doctor in Syria. Unfortunately, the stories all ended with death or destruction, people escaping in the middle of the night, and people being severely wounded. And the last few pictures she saw were that of several older men in the family standing behind younger men in various uniforms.

"So they were part of the Syrian army?"

"Not just any army. They were part of the president's detail. Some of your relatives were palace guards, a very important role. Sadly, everything has changed. Depending on how they could escape and whether or not they had family, I'm afraid most of these people are either dead or scattered to parts of the world we don't know about. And some of them could be in prison somewhere. The occupying armies rode across your territories, picking up men of military age and storing them in prison. Life as your family knew it at one time ceased to exist. Long before those final days, you were sent to the United States."

Sambra could see there was some hesitancy in the way Assad communicated those last two sentences. She picked up that perhaps there was more meaning there.

"Sent?"

One of her cousins, Viktor, blurted out, "Captured. You were captured. And taken away. You were stolen. They had no right to do that to you. Your place was with your family." The boy was filled with rage.

Ansari placed his hand on Sambra's hand tapped it. "Just like you, my dear, people's experiences of the wartimes bring up many, many unpleasant memories. These boys were mere street urchins, children roaming for food in those days, delivering messages, trying to do whatever they could to save their families. It was a very difficult time, and what they saw at a very young age obviously leaves a lasting impression." Ansari looked up to the boy who had stood and began to walk to the kitchen.

Viktor stopped and turned, gently gracing Sambra with a bow. He said, "I apologize if I offended you, my cousin. I am most grateful for your generosity in seeing us. And I am overjoyed that you wish to reunify with your family. I do not want to do anything that would interfere with that. Please accept my humble apology." And then he bowed lower still.

Sambra didn't know what to say, but she looked into the faces of the men and realized what she'd known all along. That the aftermath of war had dispersed their family all over the globe, and many of them did not survive. She'd come to know first-hand its impacts and how people live in hell afterwards and never recover.

For her, it was joyous to find some family she had left. For them, it brought up old wounds and relived tragedies.

She was going to have to figure out a way she could listen to their stories, hear their thoughts, understand their feelings, and be able to move on as best she could. She knew nothing about helping people in their situation. But she understood exactly how they felt.

CHAPTER 23

ARMANDO WAS LOOKING forward to returning to the counseling group after his coffee with Sambra. He'd had a difficult time getting her out of his mind. Several days went by, and he even considered giving her a call, asking for another get-together. But he'd been given the phone number by Kyle with tons of conditions. He had to promise not to get them all in trouble, no matter the cost to himself, and he wasn't to impose himself on her, talk to her, or try to coerce her into a meeting she didn't want to have. He'd given his word. His word was his bond.

He also took the advice of several of his teammates to just let things go natural. Let time go by, give her time to think, and allow her to adjust to the idea he was trying to help her. They all were.

He was busy too. They were compiling their African reports, and Kyle even said that a select delegation may be sent to meet with UN investigators. It was possible someone would have to go to Europe. Kyle was trying to nix that one in the bud.

"We don't do politics here," he said. "We only spend our time protecting those that do. We accompany them on trips, and we help give them background detail about some of the hotspots. But we don't do any politics. I absolutely forbid it. And I will not submit to this."

In a team meeting, Kyle had mentioned there were lots of things on the horizon, people in the government who wanted to see certain ways in which the SEALs and other Special Forces were run. He let them know, while he was always open to listening to new ideas, he didn't expect to take any advice from someone who had never put on a uniform.

He made a point to indicate that, in time, they might be having women on their Teams, and they already had women taking leadership positions every day in the Navy. That was going to continue, and they would have to embrace it. The main problem for Kyle was leadership not knowing the enemy or having a distorted vision of how to deal with the enemies of peace. Lives were at stake every day, and the world wasn't getting any safer.

"I'm heartened by the number of vets, SEALs in particular, running for office. But that's their job. That's their gig. They served the Navy or whatever branch of service they were in, and now they're done. You can't do both things while you're in the military. You can have your opinions, but no politics here. Are we clear on that, everyone?"

Tiny leaks had emerged about their mission to Africa, and a small-town reporter in rural upstate New York got wind of the atrocities. and the role the SEALs played in getting the senators over and back. He wanted to do an interview of the team.

The Navy encouraged Kyle to be the face of their team, and he declined.

Armando was thankful for this, as were many of the others.

"You guys better not write a book about this. And if you do, I was never there," Kyle said with his arms crossed his chest. He smiled, and several in the audience said, "Hooyah."

Kyle grabbed Armando's arm after the meeting and asked him how things were going. He caught him up to date on his son.

"Mom has been a real godsend. She watches Artemis all the time, and she and Gus take him places. I mean, I think he has a better life without me than he does with me. That said—"

Kyle interrupted him with a solid punch to the arm. "Knock that shit off, Armani. You know damn well that kid needs you twenty-four seven. But you know we all live in the real world, and we can't do that, can we?"

"Roger that, LT."

"So you're getting some counseling. You're feeling a little more on solid ground now that we're back, assuming we don't have to do some kind of shit show in New York or somewhere overseas. And I'm going to seriously try to not let that happen."

"No, I've been doing really well. I'm going to Brownlee's group, and I've got lots of trainings I'm doing with some of the guys coming up. I helped a couple of BUD/S instructors do a training, and you know how I love messing around with those tadpoles, just like they messed around with us."

"Well, getting even are we?"

"Ah, I'm not a vengeful man Kyle. You know that about me. But it is kind of fun to stick it to those babies. I mean you know they pee in their pants. They cry."

"As we both did."

"As we both did, agreed. So I'm going to be their witness to the fact that they went through the training, and they made it. That's what it's all about, anyway. And someday they'll get to stick it to somebody coming behind them. It's kind of a game, isn't it?"

Kyle nodded his head slowly and then stared into Armando's eyes. "It's a game all right, but a very deadly one."

"So you wanted to speak to me about something?" Armando asked.

"Well, other than to check on you, I got a call from Watkins. He's asked me to meet with an FBI agent— head of a special task force—who had been tasked with taking some photographs down here, and he wants me to sit and look at a few. He said a couple of things weren't adding up. So I thought I'd bring you along if you're free."

Armando checked his watch. "I'll just text them and let them know I'll be a little bit longer?"

"You do that."

The downtown building had the standard FBI plaque on the front. Underneath in silver letters were the words "Office of Special Investigations." They stepped into the large lobby of the refrigerator the FBI called their office building, and inquired at the uniform guard in the rotunda. They were given a visitor pass after showing their military ID and escorted up the elevator to the 10th floor.

The office was buzzing with teams of mostly younger men and women, special services agents who were combing over records and computer screens. Armando had been told previously that nearly two floors were devoted directly to cybercrime in the United States, but they also were monitoring traffic on social media sites, looking for extremist groups, or searching for evidence of some kind of a threat to public safety. It wasn't their bailiwick, or what they normally dealt with, but they were happy to be friends of the FBI, if they could be.

As they sat waiting for Agent Summers to bring them to the conference room, Armando asked Kyle, "What exactly did he say?"

"Rather cryptic, Armando. Beats me. But he wanted me specifically. He wanted the LPO SEAL Team 3. He didn't want Watkins or somebody else, at least that's what he told me. He wanted somebody who had firsthand knowledge of the team."

"And so you think somebody on the team is being investigated?"

"I have no idea."

Evan Summers was an extremely fit-looking, handsome, model-type fellow in a business suit, the perfect actor to play an FBI agent in some kind of a romance movie, Armando thought. He was overwhelmed with the guy's firm handshake, and he didn't run across many people who towered him by nearly twelve inches who was also fit and lean.

"Damn, you must lift weights or have played basketball. Those fingers, those knuckles, your hands... they're lethal weapons," Kyle said. He completely mirrored Armando's own conclusions.

Summers smiled, his hands tucked into his slacks, giving them that sly Hollywood tilt of the head type of reaction, and said, "Yeah, I get that a lot. I never played basketball. Can you believe it?"

"You're lying. I know you're lying." Kyle challenged.

All three of them laughed.

"Tennis. That's my game," Agent Summers answered.

He led them down through the busy sea of desks and into a corner glass conference room that overlooked the city of San Diego on two sides. It was one of the most impressive views Armando had ever seen.

"I see you can keep an eye on our fleet for us. We thank you for that." Said Armando.

"I'm sorry, but I wouldn't know what I was looking at, guys. My training is elsewhere. But if you're trying to say thank you, well, I think thanks needs to go to you guys. Even in the FBI, I don't run across many people who would be willing to risk their life doing the kinds of things you do. And that's why I have some questions."

Evan motioned to a couple of seats, and the two SEALs sat across the table from him.

"We got some information from a reliable source that there's a local attorney here who handles immigration disputes, and he's of Arabic descent. We believe he's from either Turkey or Iran, and we're looking into that, which is not a problem. We like to see citizens of the United States and those wishing to become citizens of the United States have representation. We don't begrudge that. But the source of the intel seems to throw some shadow on whether or not he could be operating some kind of a scheme to bring in young terrorist recruits from other countries through the student visa program."

"Well, that's been in the papers all over the place," said Kyle.

Evan nodded. "Yes, but up until now, at least in this area, most of our resources have been used in border security with Mexico, and to be honest with you, I would say three-quarters of our time is spent there. Maybe more. However, this was an outlier. This one warranted some further review. He was advertising for children of certain Middle Eastern countries who were adopted at a young age. Children from orphanages and such."

"Okay, how does that involve us?" Kyle asked.

"Again, let me say that helping to get these orphans placed is something we look upon favorably, mind you. That's not the problem. The problem is that these kids are being targeted years later, and perhaps forced or lured into doing something they wouldn't have done on their own. They are looking for recruits, we suspect."

"Wow."

Armando was beginning to feel very uncomfortable, based on the information he'd just learned from Sambra, who was adopted at a young age and had just spoken to an immigration attorney nearby.

"So I asked one of our assets if he could run a surveillance on this fellow's office in Los Angeles. To be honest with you, we don't understand how he stays in business, because he doesn't have many clients who stop by. Hardly none. So we took some shots at his home, and we found some interesting stuff. I thought I'd show you.

Evan laid out in front of them some glossy photographs of the man he identified as the immigration attorney and several other Middle Eastern-looking men.

"Now just the fact that Middle Eastern men want to get together is not a reportable incident, even though conspiracy theorists and TV reporters might think otherwise. So that's not what this is about. We looked over some of the records Mr. Assad Nefrusia—that's this man right here—," he pointed to the picture, "has handled, permitting or running applications for student visas, and we noticed something in common. We noticed that many of the student visas that he helped procure went fallow, especially the older ones.

They were submitted with applications to various colleges and even transcripts. But after a period of months, these students disappear, and they don't have any trace of whatever became of them."

"Did they find jobs? Maybe drop out and go work for someone else?" Kyle asked.

"No, when I say gone, they're MIA. No trace of them. No trace of them leaving the country. In fact, we don't even have traces of them ever entering U.S. soil to begin with. And some, a small group of them, have gotten married to these orphaned women who have grown up American but have no roots in the Middle East, and then *both* of them disappear. These are U.S. citizens too."

"So you think maybe he's bringing in people for, what?" Kyle asked.

"It's a good question, and you're right on target there, Kyle. We don't know, though. However, we did get some pictures of people we have been watching very closely while monitoring his home. Who have been involved in things in other cities in the United States, as well as in the Middle East and in Europe. Known people on our terrorist watch list. And that concerns us. That's the missing link."

"So why us, why the SEALs?"

"It's because of her."

Armando watched as the FBI special agent produced a photograph of Sambra leaving Assad Nefrusia's house. He hated his earlier suspicion was on target. He kicked himself for not asking her more about her meeting with the attorney.

"That's Sambra Gunnerson. She was married to one of our guys, Erik."

"Yeah, a guy who got popped." Evan traded off looking between Kyle and Armando.

"I know her," said Armando. "I know she's struggling, and who wouldn't?"

Kyle paused before he answered. "She's angry, maybe a little angry at the Navy, but I honestly think she married because they legitimately loved each other. They were really a love match. There was no arranged marriage here. Are you saying that she was an arranged visa holder?"

"No, no, no, Kyle. She was adopted as a baby," Armando inserted. "That couldn't have happened. But she found this attorney, and I think she did it on her own."

The agent searched Armando's face. "I'm glad you're here, and if you know her, would you be willing to get information about what she's doing?"

Armando sat back in his chair. He never thought he would ever be asked to spy on the wife of a fallen brother. He laced his fingers through his hair and turned to Kyle. "How do I answer that question, Kyle?"

"Is she suspected of breaking the law? Is her former husband suspected of this?" Kyle asked.

"Nope. We have no such belief," Agent Summers answered.

"You're asking us to spy on somebody who's grieving the loss of her husband. You're asking for us to lie to her, to talk to her under false pretenses. She already doesn't trust the Navy a whole lot, and she's dealing with her new life. I don't feel very good about this. I know you guys do this sort of thing all the time, but we stay out of this shit. And there's a reason for it. We're not capable of doing this," Kyle said.

"But what if her new life involves her getting involved in a group she perhaps doesn't even know she's getting involved with?" Evan said. "Wouldn't you then be helping her? Keeping her from making a life-changing mistake? I mean, I'm all for people going back to get in touch with their roots, but with this dude, I don't think that's really happening. She might think it is, but trust me, I don't think he's reputable." Agent Summers leaned back on his chair and waited for his words to take the proper effect.

Armando nodded and then mumbled to his hands. "Or we basically become double agents, turning her into some kind of a mole. What if we start asking her to make sacrifices she's not willing to make?"

Agent Summers had an answer for that one too. "I

agree. But there comes a time when a person has to make that decision for themselves. If you were going to get involved in something going to cause the destruction or damage to the United States or leaders or, look at it this way, against the SEALs? There have been threats on SEALs and their families for years, people who tried to get information about them from housekeepers and babysitters. You know what kind of a close community it is. And there's a reason why we don't want you running around writing books and telling people about all your exploits. First, it's not who you are, but second, it's for your own protection. But if the chips were down and you were faced with that decision, wouldn't you choose doing what will keep your teammates safe?"

CHAPTER 24

T HE GROUP MEETING started on time, but Armando hadn't shown his face yet. Sambra left the chair vacant next to her, hoping that perhaps he would join her there.

They heard the distinctive knock on the door, indicating a late arrival. And she heard Armando's voice whispering to Dr. Brownlee. The doctor allowed him to enter, then checked the hallways, and closed the door again. There were several open seats that he scanned, but Sambra smiled up at him and patted the chair next to her, indicating she wanted him to sit there. He took her up on her offer.

"So, Penny, I think you were in the middle of something? You were talking about your children, how they have grown, and how they view your new dating life. Is that correct?" Dr. Brownlee directed.

While Penny was describing how her children didn't approve of some of the men she was dating,

Armando leaned into Sambra's side and thanked her for saving the chair.

"I did it, but you did say you might be dropping out of the group, so I wasn't sure, but anyway, you're welcome." She smiled.

Both got a cool look from Dr. Brownlee, who put his forefinger up to his mouth.

Sambra couldn't help but think about all of the new things she was starting to work on. She had enrolled in a class at San Diego State in Middle Eastern history, and she was looking for restaurants and bazaars that were frequented by people from Syria and other parts of the Middle East. She'd been excited about seeing the pictures of her mother, father, and all the family members no longer living. She was extremely grateful to Assad and Ansari, and she couldn't wait to have more conversations with Khalil.

Her thoughts were interrupted when someone made a loud remark in the group.

"I'm surprised to see you guys kind of chummy today," one of the older former military men barked. He didn't appear to be particularly warm toward either one of them. "I mean, last week you two were kind of yelling at each other, back and forth, and now you're best buds. So what the hell's going on with this? I just want to know." He turned to Dr. Brownlee. "Is that a question I can ask or talk about here?"

Brownlee slowly nodded his head. "Well, it depends on if they wish to discuss it. Sambra, Armando? Do you have something to add?"

Armando took in a big gulp of air and squirmed on the chair, toying with the wedding ring he still wore on his left hand. Sambra was keenly aware of this and a little ashamed she had been focusing so much on something else outside the group. She'd not been paying attention to her fellow group mates. The man's comment annoyed her, but she also understood where it was coming from.

"Well, first—"

Armando had started to speak at the same time. "You go ahead, and then I'll talk," Armando said.

"Okay. Armando and I met for coffee, and we discussed a lot of things. It was his idea, by the way, and I'm glad that I agreed to go. I guess I should apologize to this group. I was just in a head space that... well, none of us get any training in this, do we? And I'm not as experienced with families or marriage or even group things, so I think most of the time I've been just reacting to stuff, really not thinking things through. And I want to change that. I don't want to promise that I won't be inappropriate, but I appreciate Armando taking the time and caring enough about me to help me gather my thoughts and become a more productive member, I guess."

Sambra knew she'd just blurted out drivel without thinking, and it embarrassed her. She felt like an idiot, but her nerves had gotten the better of her good judgment.

Several people in the group didn't believe her; several others did. Dr. Brownlee waved his finger and asked for the floor. She was hoping he could rescue her.

"We want to be careful with those labels. What you did wasn't necessarily bad. We learn from our mistakes. We don't want to be talking about being successful members of the group or fully participating members of the group like it's some kind of a goal to do that. We don't want to be putting a value judgment on how somebody handles their grief, either. Things come up, and some people are able to express deep, deep emotional things without getting spun out, and others can't. And it changes all the time. Now, if my grandson should take a hammer to the trunk of my antique Thunderbird, I will come undone. I will take his little butt, and I will warm it. And I'll probably feel horrible about it afterwards."

The group laughed.

"You see, in certain circumstances, we might be fine. In others, we are not going to have the ability to react in a manner that we're happy about. It's all about seeing what other people do and learning from how they recover."

Sambra thought that he did an excellent job and had definitely created a space for her to be there. She turned to Armando. "Your turn."

"I'm not sure I can give you an answer, because I don't want to reveal our private conversation. That's part of what we all agreed to," Armando started. "I've probably shared too much in this group already. But I just wanted her to know I didn't harbor any ill will toward her, and I made some suggestions to help her cope. I wanted to reassure her there are some really good ways to find yourself again, and there are some ways that are going to be full of pitfalls, accidents, and tragedies. I'd like to see everybody here find the healthiest path to healing. We'll all find different paths. And I just thought maybe, if she and I talked, we could find some common ground and get rid of some of the rancor and the animosity." He shook his head and then added, "I'm not sure if it worked, but I'm willing to try."

After the session, it was Sambra's turn to suggest they meet for coffee. Armando agreed, but he wasn't nearly as friendly as he had been the week before. He seemed pensive, thinking of work perhaps. But she had so much good news she was bursting to share with him. She tried to keep her emotions level and give him a chance to warm up.

She suggested they find the small deli she and Erik had enjoyed. They ordered their food, along with some espresso, and sat.

"I have some wonderful news, Armando."

"Really? That's good. That's really good."

The angle of his head and the way he stared at her through slitted eyes and the side of his handsome face were pleasing to her. It was the first time she had noticed this. A tiny flutter in her belly confirmed that her body was responding to him.

"I think I told you I met with an immigration attorney."

Armando nodded and took a sip of his coffee.

"Well, it turns out he has located some of my people back in Syria."

"In Syria? They live in Syria now?"

"Actually, they're scattered all over. I saw pictures of my parents and some of their brothers and sisters the store they used to have, their house. I've met my brother who has traveled here from Paris, and some cousins that are related mostly by marriage."

Armando didn't react at all.

"I've decided to take a Middle Eastern history class. I'm starting to learn about foods and customs, and I'm really jazzed about all of it. It's like there's a whole huge part of my past, my history, my bloodline I know nothing about. Now I get the chance to connect. I never dreamed I'd be so lucky. And guess what? They all want to meet me as well."

"How do you know they are your relatives?" Armando asked.

She frowned. "They had paperwork, visas, business permits, school transcripts, and the deed to my parents' house. I saw Khalil's transcripts at a school in Paris."

"Khalil? He's your brother? And he went to school in Paris? Just how does that work?" Armando asked.

"He was sent there during part of the war for his safety, because my parents and most of the rest of the family of their generation are dead. He and my other brother and I believe there's another one too—I haven't met him yet, though—that survived. And I think it's wonderful they're trying to reach out and help me understand where I came from."

Armando stared into her eyes. "I'm going to ask you something, and I don't want you to react to it." He reached across the table and took her hand in his, firmly squeezing it. "Please listen to me."

"You're scaring me, Armando."

"I want you to ask yourself if you know for sure these people are who they say they are. There are people out there who prey on widows and orphaned children. They're not nice people at all. And they can be very dangerous, Sambra."

She removed her hand from his grip. "I thought you would be happy for me," she said sharply. She could see that Armando's training, his background, and his years of combat duty in places like Syria had jaded his thinking.

"I'm only looking out for what's good for you. Promise me that you won't do anything that will jeopardize your citizenship or make you violate the law."

"What in the world are you thinking? We're talking family reunions, sharing food, and learning customs." She felt her blood pressure rising.

"Traveling to distant places to visit? Does that come up?"

"We hardly talked about travel." She could see he wasn't pleased with all that she had been doing. "Who has filled your head with such lies?"

She was ready to leave and run to her car, but as she stood, he grabbed her arm.

"Sit down. I have some things to show you. And I'm not sure if I'm doing the right thing or not, but I want you to see a couple of things. I need you to talk to a friend of mine. Will you agree?"

"What, now?"

"Right now. Exactly."

CHAPTER 25

A GENT SUMMERS ASKED them to meet him at a field office just outside of Downtown, rather than the main FBI building. Armando offered to drive Sambra there, but she insisted on driving herself.

He called Kyle on the way as he followed behind her.

"What's up, Armani?"

"I'm taking Sambra in to talk to Agent Summers."

"Already? Man, you move fast."

"Well, she said some things to me that were disturbing, and I felt ill-equipped to be able to explain to her some of the information he gave us, Kyle. I thought it best that he do the communications. But I have all kinds of regrets and doubts. I really don't want to be here."

"I get you. And thanks for checking in. I'm sorry, but you're kind of stuck with this one. And, however it goes, I think you did the right thing. Sometimes we aren't sure, are we?"

Armando was continually grateful for his LPO's leadership.

"Ask me to sight someone's long gun, ask me to estimate where's the fire, ask me where's the best place to seek cover, ask me anything about scopes or halo drops or training exercises, and I can give you enough information to fill a library. But this stuff, this interpersonal stuff, is just not something I'm comfortable with. And if she doesn't take well to this information, what have I done? I've just destroyed her life."

"You honestly think that's what's going to happen? I mean, based on some of the things you've heard, based on what she's already told you, don't you think the FBI's correct?"

"Yes, I do have faith in them. I just am not sure how she's going to take it. And that's what I'm fearing."

"Well, you're going to know in just a little while, so call me afterwards, okay?"

"You got it."

He pulled up next to Sambra's car and opened the door for her, which led to a hallway with several interview rooms leading off to the right and the left. A door opened at the end of the hall, and Agent Summers appeared and walked down to greet them.

"Thank you for agreeing to see me, Sambra. And thanks to you, too, Armando, for setting this up.

Sambra, I'm going to show you some things that might be disturbing. Let's head back to the office."

They both followed him several feet until Summers stopped, turned, and addressed Armando. "If you would like, you can take off, or you can stay. It's up to you."

Armando was relieved. "That sounds good to me. I'll leave you to it then." To Sambra, he said, "You call me if you need to, okay?" She looked like a scared little girl.

"I'd feel better if you stayed. I mean that," she whispered.

Armando was surprised at her reaction. "If you're sure." His urge to leave her in Agent Summer's capable hands was strong, but there was a part of him that didn't want to abandon her.

"I'm sure."

Armando's relief evaporated. He knew he was stuck, and he knew he had to stay.

"All right then, let's get this done," Summers said, quietly.

Once seated behind the Formica-top table, Summers pulled out of his briefcase several brown folders marked with notes, each bearing the FBI seal. He began with an explanation before he opened the first file.

"We've started a task force looking into specific irregularities around certain known individuals who are suspected of being involved in terrorism and terrorism threats, either in the United States or elsewhere. Of course, the FBI is mainly concerned with threats to our population, like public safety issues within the U.S. borders. But oftentimes our research goes further."

Summers unfolded his hands and began opening the first folder.

"In this particular case, your attorney friend, Assad Nefrusia, has been flagged as a known associate of people we know for sure had some connection to terrorist events in Europe. More specifically in France, Belgium, and the UK."

Sambra's color left her face. Armando could see the top of her chest shaking as her inhale and exhale became ragged. Her lips formed a straight line, without smile or frown. Her fear was written all over her.

"You're sure about this information?" she asked. Her voice wavered.

"As sure as we can be. We've photographed people coming and going from Nefrusha's office and house. That's how come we identified you. You're not under suspicion, Sambra, but we thought perhaps you could help us obtain more information about this group. Something that might help us clarify their intent, and in the outside chance they are just innocents doing a humanitarian good deed, we could rule them out. But we wouldn't be coming to you talking to you about it if we didn't believe they are threats to our Homeland."

"Threats to the U.S.?"

"Yes, ma'am."

"But surely you have teams who take care of these things. Even if I did believe you, I still don't understand what you're asking of me."

Armando was proud of her strength.

Agent Summers pulled out several pictures of terrorist bombings in several European cities. "These are pictures of what we believe they have been up to. Perhaps not all of the attacks, but they are suspected in most. There was a bombing on a subway station just outside of London and two bombings in France—one at the port of Nice and one just outside of Paris. Plus, there's been another bombing at a military recruitment center in Belgium. Some of these, for purposes of national security, have not been widely disclosed."

She scanned the photos, not daring to touch any of them, her eyes welling with tears.

He informed her of the casualty count, and he showed pictures of individuals who had been seen at the sites before the bombs had been detonated. Agent Summers tapped a finger on the photograph of a man carrying a backpack, turning to look over his shoulder.

"Do you know this man?" he asked.

Sambra looked over the photograph, her hand

coming up to her mouth as tears rolled freely down her cheeks.

"Yes, I know this man. I've had dinner with him. This is Ansari Timur. He's a friend of Mr. Nefrusia. He's the gentleman who told me he'd found members of my family."

"Good. Thank you. Okay, and do you recognize any of these individuals?"

Sambra looked over six other photos, shaking her head as she scanned the first five, but on the sixth one, she once against covered her mouth.

"Oh my God. They told me that this is Khalil, my brother. So you think my brother is involved in this as well?"

"Sambra, as difficult as it may be to understand or grasp this, we think they all are. I wish it weren't so. But the fact that these same people are gathering together here in the San Diego, Los Angeles area, added to the fact that we have received intel of an event that may occur in California sometime in the next few months, well, these are just two coincidences that we can't ignore. We also are aware of the fact that Mr. Nefrusia has been advertising for foreign-born adopted children, just like yourself. And we're asking, did he try to recruit you?"

"No, not to recruit me. He merely told me that he could find my family. And I'm curious about them. I never signed onto any of this, bombings or terrorist acts. No one's ever talked about these things or how I feel about them."

"Of course not. They wouldn't do that, would they?" Agent Summers said. "They are good at recruiting people who think they're doing something innocent. Then it turns into something else, and then people get in so far that they can't get out. Or someone they care about is being threatened. These are not nice people, Sambra. No matter how they appear to you. There are many, many good immigrants from the Syria and other places who are solid citizens, who came because they love this country's freedom and love the U.S., even though they miss their own. But they would never participate in something like this. And as a matter of fact, that's how we were tipped off to Mr. Nefrusia's activities. He is known within the Syrian community as being someone who cannot be trusted. Were you aware of that?"

"No, I was not."

"We need to find out what it is they're planning. And I have to ask if you would be willing to help us."

"Help you? You mean like spy for you?"

Armando saw how uncomfortable she was. At such a young age, this was quite a bit to dump on her shoulders. He felt bad that he had allowed her to get involved.

"I'm asking for your help," Agent Summers said. "I don't have the right to, but I don't know any other way to get a full list of their contacts, how they operate, or anything at all that you could tell us about them. And in the process, we will take special care to watch out for you, to make sure that you are kept safe. If at any time you feel uncomfortable in this situation, you just let us know, and we take you out. But we really feel you could be of great benefit in helping us solve what it is they're planning."

Sambra looked down to her lap and then spoke. "Mr. Nefrusia's wife and two children, I think, are planning a trip, that's all I know. But I don't know where they're going. No one has ever talked about anything like staging an attack or going after somebody. I mean, we've only talked about families, and I've seen pictures of where my family lived, the village, the house my parents lived in. That's all."

"All to gain your trust. I doubt very much that any of those photographs are pictures of your real family. And I wish I could tell you otherwise. But if you want to learn more about the culture you were born into, there are many groups living very close by that would be happy to accept you and teach you about what it would've been like to have been raised there instead of raised where you were. In Portland."

"Are you completely sure that Khalil, Ansari Timur, and Fazra are involved?"

"You have met Fazra Bonsil?" Agent Summers asked.

"Yes."

"He's a bomb maker, Sambra. A very gifted and brilliant bomb maker. That only further cements my suspicions."

Sambra closed her eyes, bowed her head, and sobbed, "What did I do to ever deserve getting involved in all this? All I wanted to do was get married, have a family, and live a normal life. All I wanted was to find somebody to love me. And I did. And then when he was taken away, I discovered this chance to find the people who missed me, the people who gave me up so I could have a relationship with those who had been lost to me. It was a miracle they were offering me. Whatever the circumstances. I thought of them fondly, that they were giving me a fresh start. And now what you're showing me is devastation and death."

"No, there are many trusted individuals from your former country who we work very closely with. These people," he said as he tapped the pile of photos, "are predators. And they are very good at it. But the people who can really teach you about your family's culture, they're not here in these photographs. And we can help and introduce you to people who would be willing to show you. But right now, our immediate problem and my immediate request is to ask you for your help. Will you help us?"

She turned and looked at Armando. "Is this something I should do? Would you advise that I do this? Isn't this the kind of risk you guys take all the time?"

Armando nodded his head. "It's your decision, and I would be lying if I said it was without risk. But on the other hand, think of the innocent people who might be saved if you can help them solve this puzzle. Then you will have been a force for good. That's what Erik was all about, Sambra. He became a SEAL to be a force for good, an action hero, if you will. And he'd be very proud of you, I think, if you helped the FBI with this search. I know I would, if I were in his shoes."

He watched her examine his face and hoped she didn't pick up his unintended meaning the wrong way. For someone so young, she was growing up fast. She was strong, but she was also still extremely naive.

"I will help you, however much you want me to, Sambra," he added. "I may not be able to do much, but I can help keep you safe, if allowed, if you need me. But I cannot interfere with their work. You need to understand that. That's the FBI's job."

"I do understand," she said, nodding. "And it means a lot to me, Armando. I just might take you up on that."

The day had started out for Armando with the

team meeting, then a meeting with the FBI, and a group counseling session afterwards. And now this. In a million years, he never would've guessed that a day could have been so jam-packed with emotion, danger, and resolve. But one thing was for sure, he wasn't going to let her walk in without some kind of a backup plan. And if it meant he had to step over the line a bit to protect her, he had an enormous urge to do so.

He only hoped that he didn't lose his Trident in the process.

He was fairly sure he was about to lose his heart.

CHAPTER 26

S AMBRA SHED HER clothes, drew a nice hot bath, added some lavender salts, and laid back in the foamy water, hoping to soak away some of the thoughts and feelings welling up inside, overwhelming not only her brain but her heart as well.

She closed her eyes and thought about all that had occurred that day. All the ups and downs she'd gone through, the gamut of emotions from happiness to questions about her future, her concerns about loyalty and who to trust. Maybe if she was ten years older she could handle these things no problem. Now, faced with all of the possibly bad decisions she'd made, she wasn't sure she could.

She saw the faces of everybody she had talked to that day. Starting with Khalil, the cousins, Armando, Dr. Brownlee, and then Agent Summers. In her mind, each of their pictures flashed by one by one until she rested on Armando's face.

Of all the people she'd seen and talked to, Armando's expression was one that seemed to have the bright light behind it, the kind features of a man who cared for her, just like her husband had up until his death.

Be careful, Sambra. Be careful about rushing to judgment, making decisions that are going to ruin your life.

When it came to planning her future—attending school, leaving her family unit, and moving to San Diego years ago—of all those decisions, the best one was her choice from her heart, marrying Erik. He had been her stalwart for almost two years. Not nearly enough to time to explore that relationship, to let it bloom inside her and heal all the scars, but it had been one of the most stable and happy times of her life. Her insights were sometimes a jumbled mess. But Erik could do what she needed to have done. He'd soothed her soul. He'd given her what she'd always wanted. He was her protector, and she had thought he always would be there.

And he would have.

She remembered the day when Gina told her that she would find love again. She couldn't decide then if that was a true statement. She didn't believe her. Now, as she studied Armando in her mind—sitting in the sunlight from the window, on his cell phone, as he drove away in his truck, as he sat and listened, not touching her but sitting close to her in the agent's office—she liked the feeling of calm it brought her life. His warmth. His voice was kind, and he was patient, so much older than Erik. She thought he gave wise counsel.

Is the council Assad and Ansari were giving wise? Or were they, just like Agent Summer said, working off of her frailties, her desire to discover and explore her roots.

What Agent Summers asked her to believe and what Armando underscored was important. It wasn't that she couldn't have roots or a community or acquaintances with people who could teach her about her family's language and culture, but she should be careful who she chose to follow. She hadn't even considered researching this until she saw the newspaper ad.

So how stupid is that? She fell for a newspaper advertisement! Was she going to base her whole future on that? Or her desire for connection?

And then there was that pause when Armando lingered by her car. She wished she'd let him drive, and again, he offered to take her home. That was an easy answer.

"No. I'm going to go home and have a nice long bath and go to bed early. But thank you."

There was more she wanted to say, but there were no words to express everything that she felt.

And then she tried.

"Armando, I am so sorry for what I have put everybody through."

"No need to say that, Sambra. It's not necessary."

"But it is. I have been a complete idiot, a fool. I've been a child. And that's exactly the opposite of what I want to do with the rest of my life. I've been stuck in all this negativity and living in a room with rose-colored glasses, not seeing what was clearly right in front of me all along. I would like to say I've been wrong about my assessments, these men, and their alleged schemes. But the two of you have helped me understand I was about to jump off a ledge, and perhaps there would be no return. What I want to ask you, Armando, is whether you'll be my friend? Will you help me to find the clarity I need?"

He didn't say anything at first. She feared she'd offended him.

"Of course, sweetheart," he said as his hand came up to her cheek. "I am here for you. I feel just as responsible as you do about all this. It's not fate, Sambra, that we met each other. It's something that I feel like I've been called to do. I wouldn't abandon you, and I would like you to trust me."

She'd taken his hand in hers and laid her cheek against it again. "Thank you."

She turned because she needed to think about what

was going on inside her heart. She had no right to expect or want some kind of relationship other than friendship with Armando. And she knew she needed something. But she didn't want that need to be him. She wanted to come to him strong. Not from the place of weakness.

As she drove away, he waved. She nearly pulled over and ran to his arms, but that wasn't wise.

The bathtub water was getting cooler. She added a little more hot to the mix, smoothed salts off her body, added oils, and then stepped out of the tub. Wrapped in a large towel, she headed for the bedroom when she heard a knock on her door.

"Armando," she whispered.

Excitement coursed through her veins. She was not presentable, she was in a bath towel, naked underneath. But she ran to her door anyway and opened it without thinking.

Ansari forced himself through the four inches of space she gave him. He glared at her standing wet and naked under the large towel. Behind him stood two strangers. And then Khalil entered, his eyes still downcast.

"Go get yourself presentable," Ansari said in a guttural nasty voice.

"But what are you doing here?"

"What do you think, Sambra?"

She had no idea he knew where she lived or that he suspected she'd been in contact with the FBI. But of course, if he really was who Agent Summers and Armando told her he was, he would know that. He would've checked on that. Again, she felt so stupid at being so naive.

"What is this all about? Get out of my apartment. Get out of my house."

"You're going to take a little trip. And nothing is going to happen to you if you cooperate, but you're going to come with us. We have something we need you to do."

"But it's night. I was just getting ready for bed."

Ansari nodded toward her bedroom, "Check the room, check all the closets." Then he turned and asked her, "Are you alone, my dear? Or are you perhaps expecting someone?"

"Of course not. I'm going to bed early."

"Not right now." He gave her an evil grin. "Get your clothes on. Dress warmly."

Khalil whispered in Ansari's ear. "Where is her cell phone?"

"It's charging in the kitchen." She purposely lied, directing them to Erik's cell phone, still plugged into the charger. She'd never had the heart to throw it away.

Khalil disconnected the black case and handed it to Ansari. "Now, I said get dressed, and I'm not waiting more than five minutes. If you don't get ready now, I will take you naked."

One of the strangers wandered over to the bedroom door and gestured with his hand. As she went inside and began taking clothes out of her dresser, her towel still firmly wrapped around her body, she asked him, "Are you going to stand there and watch me?"

He leered at her, and his eyes followed the trail from her feet all the way up the towel to her neck and then her face. And then he slowly glanced back down again. She could tell his intentions were completely evil.

"You are only delaying things if you stand there and watch me. I will not dress or undress in front of you." The man stepped toward her, raising his arm as if to slap her. Khalil stopped him.

"I will watch. You go."

And he did just that. He stood in the doorway his back to her.

Sambra had her cell phone in the back pocket of her jeans, which had been deposited next to the bed when she undressed. She took those jeans and a fresh pair of underwear and sat ostensibly to put them on. While she did so, she scrolled the recent contacts to find the number Armando had called her from. She texted H and then H again and then H all the way across the screen then slipped the cell under her pillow and put on the rest of her clothing. At last, she added running shoes and socks. She got a ponytail holder from the bathroom and then clipped her hair on top of her head.

"I'm going to get a jacket now," she said. Inside her closet was one of Erik's big jackets, as she called it. It smelled like him, and it gave her hope. On the outside was the distinctive insignia of the Navy SEALs, the Trident, the eagle, and the pistol.

She picked up her purse, not adding her cell phone, and declared herself ready.

Ansari grabbed her arm in a grip that she knew was going to cause bruises. Someone from behind roughly put a white cloth sack over her head.

And then there was a horrible smell of something like disinfectant shoved up under the sack, placed around her nose. Black spots appeared in the corners of her eyes, and she lost her balance but had no recollection of falling.

"God help me. Help me." she whispered.

It was the last thing she heard.

CHAPTER 27

A RMANDO'S CELL PHONE pinged, and the screen lit up with Sambra's message. The letters H repeated all the way across the line of text.

He feared that only meant one thing, that she was in trouble. He dialed Agent Summers.

"I think Sambra's in trouble. I just got a text from her, all H's. I think she means help."

"Yes, we are following them," Summers answered.

"Them? You had her followed? You have her under surveillance?"

"Of course, it's what we do. It's SOP."

"I want to be involved."

"That's not the agreement, Armando. You know that."

"Well then, tell me where they are, and I want to be there when you have her. I must be there."

"Relax, Armando. It's under control. We are monitoring, and I will let you know what happens, as I can.

You know these things are practiced and set up in advance. We have a way we do it, just like you do. Now you need to let me do my job. Because while I'm on the phone, I'm not getting messages from my field agents."

"I apologize, but I insist. Are you in the office?"

"I am, but you cannot come here. I would say wait at home, and I will let you know when and if you can help."

"You're following people who have taken her somewhere? She is going unwillingly, right? I mean, you don't think—?"

"You need to calm down. If she texted you a string of H's, what do you think?"

Armando's stomach was churning, the veins in his neck hurt they were so strained. He had never felt so helpless in his life. "Isn't there *something* I can do? Give me something, dammit!"

After a brief pause, Summers answered. "Armando, you can get ready. You can get ready to comfort her if and when we find her. But other than that, I will not have you interfering with this investigation or the apprehension of these individuals. And if you don't let me do my job, they're going to slip away. So get off the phone and stay home."

It wasn't anything Armando wanted to hear. He next dialed Kyle and, when he didn't reach him, left a message. He dialed Fredo and Cooper and spoke to both of them.

Fredo was quite disturbed. "Fuck that shit. Does she have a GPS on her phone?"

"I have no idea. I don't have access to that. I have her number. Can you do it?"

"No. It's more complicated than that. So are you just supposed to sit there and wait?" Fredo asked.

"That's what he said."

"Do you know where she lives?"

"I do not. I think Kyle knows. But he's not answering."

"Let me see if I can get hold of Watkins. He may be able to give her address, but I'm not sure. I will call you back."

Cooper was his normal laid back and sarcastic self. "Armani, these guys at the FBI are outstanding. They are better trained to handle this sort of thing. You know we used to go after guys here in the States all the time in the old days, right?"

"Yep."

"We were damned lucky we didn't get caught. Well, we can't do that shit anymore. And I think your agent guy, whoever the hell he is, I hope he's a senior agent or—"

"Special agent on the terrorism taskforce." Armando added.

"Okay, so these guys, they train for this just like we

do for other things. Get out of their way. And Kyle would not be happy if he knew you were trying to insert yourself."

There was a long pause on the phone, and then Coop added, "I told you not to get involved in this thing, if you'll remember. And I told you to be very careful, because this sort of stuff can get slippery very easily. You're not thinking with your brain. You're thinking with your heart. And while that's admirable, you got a blind spot there. And you're vulnerable. I'm speaking to you as your sometimes medic doctor when you let me. Don't do something stupid that you will regret or that will make it so you lose your Trident. And I'm giving you the advice that Kyle would tell you if he was available."

"I understand, but I can't just let her be taken."

"And you have the right guys on the job, Armani. You helped do that. Don't forget that. You've already helped by getting her in touch with the FBI. So quit being a baby and step back and wait. And I know it sucks. Do I have to come over and babysit you, because I was just about to sit down to the most fantastic dinner Libby has ever cooked. It's steak and French fries. She just pulled it off the barbecue. I was going to have myself an ambrosia of a dinner then ice cream and pie for dessert. Do I have to come over there babysit your ass and miss all that?"

"No."

"Goddammit, I'll be there in ten minutes. Don't you move a muscle."

By the time Cooper arrived at Armando's home, he still hadn't heard from Kyle. But he had called his mother and asked her to keep Artemis for overnight. The last thing in the world he wanted was for his son to be involved in some kind of operation that might be run out of his house. As unlikely as that sounded, he just wanted Artemis safe and in the arms of his mother. That's the way Gina would have wanted it.

Coop sauntered into the room, bringing a hamburger in a brown paper bag and drink. He handed them to Armando. "Eat. You've got to eat."

"You actually stopped at a hamburger place and picked this up?"

Coop defiantly stood in front of him and put one hand on his hip. He set the hamburger bag and the drink on the table. "*This* was my dinner. This was what I bought on the way home. Libby's out with the girls. She's got the kids."

"You fucking asshole. You lied about that steak dinner."

"Yeah, well, I really didn't want to come over. But that was foolish. I'm done. You're sitting and eating that hamburger right now, and then we're going to bide our time and wait for news. We'll do what we do after."

Armando cut the hamburger in half and gave the other portion to Cooper. They ate in silence. "What's in this?" Armando asked as he held the drink up and shook it.

"Mineral water. What did you expect?"

"Then it's for you. I'm grabbing a beer."

"Armani, I'm going to have to insist, you need to keep your wits about you, no beer. I don't want any shots, or anything, I want you just stone-cold sober. Now tell me everything that went on. I'm dying to hear what the agent told you."

As Armando explained all the events of the meeting this afternoon, Kyle returned his call.

"So what's the emergency?" Kyle asked.

"Summers is on it. I guess, Sambra had texted me a warning, a message. And Summers has somebody following her. Apparently, she's been taken, but the FBI is on top of it. So I'm sitting on my hands here. Coop's with me. Fredo's trying to get her address, and—"

"And you're not going to go over to her house. You hear me, Armani? You're going to stay right there, just like the FBI told you to. I'm not going to have you interfere with this."

Kyle had shouted into the phone, and Cooper, sitting on the other side of the table, could hear every word. He gave Armando a Cheshire cat grin and nodded.

"Well, I was just trying to see if there was something I could find, something in her house that might indicate where she was going. Or where she'd been taken."

"And then you'd be messing with evidence. And that would be something that could get you drawn up on charges, Armani. Be smart. Wait. And I know that's not what you want to do. But you got to wait. You keep me informed."

"Okay, but keep your phone on you."

"Will do."

IT TOOK NEARLY two hours, almost to nine o'clock at night, before they heard anything further from Agent Summers. Someone from his staff asked Armando to come into the field office where he had been with Sambra that afternoon. He and Cooper left immediately. He texted Kyle on the way and tried to call Fredo but had no luck.

The office was lit up as if the interior was on fire. Every single side office held two or three individuals sitting at computer terminals. People were faxing and sending photos, organizing files. There were pictures posted on a bulletin board that ran from one corner to the other in a big meeting room. The taskforce had nearly forty people working in this location tonight. Armando was duly impressed.

As they were ushered to the back room, Cooper added, "See what I mean? We don't have those kinds of assets. I hope to God this is going to be good news, but I don't think we'd be brought here if it wasn't. Obviously, they need something."

Armando nodded his agreement.

Summers was nowhere to be found, but they were shown a private interview room and a bright young agent with an ATF badge on her lapel sat in front of them and placed a recorder in the center of the table.

"I know this is something that might make you nervous, but I just want to record exactly what you told Agent Summers and why you're concerned for Sambra's health or safety."

"When are you talking—"

"Tonight, when you called him. What did you say?" She was persistently annoying.

Armando looked at the tape recorder as she turned it on with a red light flashing.

"She sent me this message." He held up his cell phone with the string of H's across the bar. "I took this to mean 'help.' I took this to mean that she didn't have time to spell out words or say anything else. She just contacted me with an H and I just know she was reaching for help. I had told her I would. And I want to now."

"And you are, by cooperating with me."

"So where is Summers?"

"I don't think I have to stress that Agent Summers is busy. Can we leave it at that?"

"Yes, ma'am." Armando was sporting a bad attitude, and he knew he had to reel it in quick.

"Okay, and after you met with Agent Summers this afternoon, then what was your conversation with Sambra?"

"Well, she was stunned. She was quiet, but in the few words that we did share, she seemed grateful that the information had been brought to her."

"Did she appear to be surprised? Or in any way sympathetic to some terrorist cause?"

"I'm a fairly good judge of character, and I don't think that's the side of the fence she came down on. She thanked me, apologized for causing so much trouble, and said she needed to wrap her mind around all of this. It seemed completely normal to me."

"Did she seem overly upset or angry?"

Armando sat back in the chair and began to focus on the young agent's demeanor. "Excuse me, but am I a suspect in this situation or am I someone you think might have undercut your investigation? Or are you looking to her as being an active willing participant in this group's activities?"

"I'm not implying anything. I'm trying to establish what the truth is. We have assets working on this, and I want to make sure that we have them adequately protected."

"Well, pardon me, but what about Sambra? Who's protecting her?"

"At the present time, they're being followed by very experienced detail teams. And I can't say anything more than that. That's what you've been told, and that's all we're able to advise at this point. The purpose of you being brought here is to ensure that you do not interfere with this mission. I'm going to ask that you remain here voluntarily. I want all your calls monitored and recorded here, and I want to make sure there isn't anything that comes to you that we don't see. And that means everything."

Armando shook his head. "Wow. I just hope you're focused on the right person, ma'am. I hope to God somebody good is looking after her. I have no way of doing so. I don't even know where she lives. But if I did, I'd be looking for clues over there."

"We've had her under surveillance for several days now. It's under control, Mr. Guzman. We just want to make sure that we don't get any interference or create anything out of our control."

She turned off the tape recorder, grabbed it, and left the room.

Cooper leaned into the table, "Well, I'm glad I brought that hamburger. But in a couple of hours, I'm going to be hungry again, because I think we just got locked into this fucking room Armando. Thanks a lot."

"But they didn't take your cell phone, Coop, so why don't you call Libby and then see if you can get hold of Fredo? Let them know. I'm under surveillance. You and I are sittin' here under surveillance."

CHAPTER 28

S AMBRA OPENED HER eyes, but there was no light outside. Then she remembered someone had put a white cloth bag over her head.

My head. My head hurts. She wanted to touch a knob that hurt at the back of her head, but when she tried to lift her arm, she discovered her hands were tied at the wrist with a zip tie. Then she attempted to sit up and discovered her ankles were also bound with a zip tie.

She was helplessly in the dark, incapacitated, and riding in the back of some kind of a vehicle. Now she began to hear other sounds like clinging pieces of equipment, metal rubbing together, the sounds of cars passing them on a roadway, horns honking, and an occasional pounding earth rumble from a big truck. It hurt to think because her headache felt like somebody had jabbed a red, hot poker in the back of her skull.

Then she remembered that she had inhaled some

substance, which had forced her to go unconscious. *Must have fallen and landed on the floor hard.*

Her shoulders also hurt, so did the joints in her elbows and knees, and the back of her head pulsed.

Rocking back and forth from side to side, she felt like she was stuck in some kind of a chrysalis or cocoon. And the more she shoved pieces of equipment out of the way, the more noise she began to create.

"Where am I?" she whispered. The sound of her own scared and raspy voice alarmed her, echoing off the metal walls of the van.

Thinking about what Ansari had said before they'd put the bag over her head, she got the impression he was going to take her somewhere, possibly somewhere to kill her. He'd asked, "Did you think you could get away with it?" Whatever the hell that meant.

But now she was certain that all the suspicions Armando and Special Agent Summers brought up, all of them appeared to be true. She was in the hands of people who were not honest and seemed desperate. In fact, she saw they were the type of people who would commit violence or some act of terror. They were capable of planting a bomb or disrupting peaceful lives.

Think, Sambra, think. Think about what you can do.

She didn't have her cell phone with her, and they had Erik's phone. She had no light, she couldn't see through the cloth, and she was tied up. But she could move from side to side, and she could kick things, but she just didn't understand what she might be kicking.

She still had her running shoes on, and thank God she had the large SEAL jacket on, or she would've been cold.

The rumbling continued, so she began feeling with her feet what could be in the van with her. She tapped one metal object, which appeared to be a can, like a paint can. She moved, exploring several others and found what felt like a role of twine, perhaps a paintbrush, a hose, a hammer, and something that could be an ax although she couldn't quite tell if it was sharp or not. But it had a metal head on it, and it had a wooden handle. She could tell by how it moved and what it sounded like when she tapped against it.

She decided to focus on the ax that was her best way to get herself untied. Moving her legs over the end of what she hoped was a blade, she picked up the object with her heels and balanced her ankles on the edge. First, she applied all her weight to see if somehow the ax was sharp enough to bust through the zip tie. When that failed, she began a sawing motion back and forth in one-inch movements, and by the fourth or fifth movement, the zip tie burst open.

It wasn't freedom yet, but it gave her hope.

Next, she was going to have to try to get her hands

over to the sharp edge so she could remove the zip tie between her wrists. That turned out to be a little easier than before, since her legs helped brace her and push with her butt until she was close to where the blade was. She was able to feel the handle and the metal blade with her fingers, and again, with short sawing motions went back and forth several times and finally felt the zip tie released. She also felt that she had cut herself on her forearm, and the sting was significant. She smelled blood, including the pungent smell of the blood on the metal blade especially.

The next thing she did was remove her hood, using it to dab the cut on her forearm. The bleeding appeared to stop, but there still remained a slice in her skin she knew would reopen with little force.

The van was dark, without windows, but around the rear door where the seams were, she could see little slivers of flickering headlights, which shed some light on the contents of the van. She'd been right about the hose, and there wasn't one can like she originally thought. There were six paint cans. She also saw an alarm clock, several rolls of wire, and a box that scared her to death. On the outside of several cardboard boxes the size of her normal book box deliveries, there were red diamond designs, with letters painted in Arabic. Even though she couldn't read it, she knew full well that the boxes contained some kind of explosive.

So basically, Sambra realized, she was located inside a moving bomb with enough explosives and chemicals to take out not only herself, but probably the drivers of the van and several others on the roadway. She could imagine the pictures from a police or news chopper, with a smoking crater below three times the size of the van and no visible remnants that she had ever been there.

Gotta stop that thinking. That isn't going to help, Sambra. She wondered what Armando or Erik would do in this situation. She wished she'd had some sort of training for this.

Next, she focused on the cans. She tried to pry one open with her fingers and was unsuccessful until she found a screwdriver nearby. At first, she tried to pry the lid open and then thought better of it.

What if it's a toxic substance? What if I just poison myself if I open this thing up?

The bottom line was that she didn't know what to do. So caution told her to wait until she was sure.

A small red light flashed at a distance, the pinhole flash making her feel safer, but it was a long ways away. Then she heard sirens. In response, the driver of the van, she presumed either Assad or Ansari, sped up. She lost her balance and fell to the floor, hitting her head against the side.

She touched the back of her head, and it felt matted, caked with blood. Holding her fingers in front of her, she felt the texture and determined it was wasn't new blood, but blood that she'd suffered early on, which had now dried. She checked her ankles, her wrists, her knees, her shoulders, any place that was sore either from the zip ties or being bumped around in the van and couldn't determine that anything was broken or strained. And that made her happy. Her arms and legs free, her head uncovered, her eyes unmasked and seeing very small slashes of light through the back door, it was better than nothing. If the van stopped and the drivers came around to open the door, her job would be to pounce on them when they least expected it. So that required she be quiet.

One thing she wasn't going to do was unlatch the door, exposing herself to the traffic she could hear behind them, winding up being some kind of pathetic road kill.

The siren blared louder and louder, and then she heard a second siren. A third started from the opposite direction, and she realized they were traveling on some kind of a roadway that was not just a two-lane but possibly a four-lane highway. The van was passing cars and swerving, and drivers on either side of the van honked in protest. She knew his erratic driving was going to draw attention, and if the sirens weren't being used to chase him, they would soon pick up his behavior and perhaps force him to stop. But she just didn't know how long it would take.

As the sounds got louder and louder, the driver began to make erratic decisions. She could feel his panic. His wheels locked occasionally as he swerved. Gravel pinged under the tires and frame as he pulled on a shoulder and then righted himself, sometimes overcorrecting the van before coming back on the roadway. In short, he was driving at intense rates of speed and not very safely.

There was nothing she could do but wait and brace herself for an eventual confrontation, hoping the element of surprise would be on her side, but not understanding when the opportunity would present itself. She prayed he was a good enough driver to avoid getting into an accident.

All of a sudden, she heard a loud boom as a large vehicle rammed into the back of the van. The driver was losing control. They were spinning to the right then to the left. He braked and then released the brakes before hitting the gas. Then she heard a crunch as the front end of the van broke through some kind of fence onto another roadway. Her ears were filled with a cacophony of blaring horns as the van began to dodge between oncoming traffic, and eventually clipped the back of a vehicle and then stopped forward motion, beginning to spin in a circle. Just before the van stopped moving, something very large impacted the shell.

Sambra was thrown against the back door, as she felt a sharp pain in her leg. She tried to keep conscious. The pain was excruciating. There was the smell of smoke, and she felt warmth beneath the undercarriage of the van. She realized, to her horror, the van was on fire.

And she was trapped in the back of it.

All of a sudden, a large semi truck's horn blasted, hitting another vehicle nearby, forcing it closer to the van, where both vehicles crushed into their van.

Thank God the impact probably put out the fire.

How long will it be before I'll bleed to death?

And then there were no more thoughts.

CHAPTER 29

COOPER'S PHONE RANG.

"Hello," he answered.

Armando could hear Fredo's voice, asking for him.

"You found something, Fredo?" Armando asked.

"Kyle's coming to get you. He was livid when he found out you'd been detained. But there's a further development."

Armando was eager to get the news. "Did they find her? Have they caught them? Is Sambra okay?"

"Yes, yes, and a no."

Armando felt like his stomach dropped to the floor and rolled into the corner. "What is it, Fredo? You have to tell me. Please."

"This is really shitty, and I didn't want to have to be the one to tell you, but there's been a horrible accident. The van Sambra was riding in has been badly fucked up. Let's just say that—and we know there's some fatalities—we don't know if one is Sambra, but we don't think so. We think she is at Scripps. They took the survivors to Scripps."

Armando jumped to his feet, ran to the door, and rattled the locked handle. Screaming at the top of his lungs, he banged the door and shoved it to force an opening with his shoulders. "Goddammit, let me out of this place!"

Cooper was there in a flash, rescuing his phone so it wouldn't become a casualty as well. Armando heard Cooper whispering to Fredo as he continued to shout and scream and ask for help.

After several minutes, Armando's knuckles were bloodied. He had managed to put several cracks in the door trim, but the metal door remained whole. He wiped his knuckles on his jeans, swore, picked up one of the chairs, and started throwing in at the door over and over and over again.

Someone on the other side shouted, "Hold on. Stand back. We're opening now."

Then Armando heard the voice of his LPO, Kyle Lansdowne. He was overjoyed.

"Kyle, get me the fuck out of here. Sambra has been in an accident." The door opened, and Armando saw the ashen face of his LPO, standing there with a somber expression, just like the expression TJ had at the hospital when they brought Gina in.

"We've got to go now, Armani. I want you to come

with me; Coop, you can take his car back to his place, or you can ride with us either way."

"If it's all the same with you, I'm going to hang in there until this is over. We'll get the truck another time."

All three of them ran to Kyle's Hummer. Agents from the FBI staff stared, their mouths hanging open, shocked at the display. But the young woman who had interrogated Cooper and Armando was the very same person who had unlocked the door. She didn't look happy, but she was obviously pleased Armando was not going to be her problem any longer.

They hopped in Kyle's Hummer and tore out from the parking lot.

"We're going to Scripps," Kyle said. "Wish I didn't, but goddammit, I know exactly how to get there." He focused on the roadway, then added, "You sit back and try to relax. You're going to need all your strength. Coop, can you call ahead and see maybe if you can find out something? What did Fredo say?"

"He said she was hurt, that there were fatalities, and they didn't know if Sambra was one of them."

"Where did he get that from?"

"He said he got it from Gus Mayfield. I guess they called him after the traffic accident. And Gus tried to call Armando but gave Fredo the next call."

Thank goodness for helping cops.

IN THIRTY MINUTES, they were racing into the emergency room. Armando knew the score and confronted the security guard at the reception desk, who allowed him to go to the back with Cooperand, one of the male orderlies. He looked to see if he could find a doctor or a nurse or somebody he could get information from. Instead, all he saw was rows of patients, some on gurneys, some in wheelchairs. Orderlies and janitorial staff mopped up floors and moved things around. The area was packed with people and not enough rooms to see them in. The orderly brought them to an emergency desk, and the nurse in charge greeted them.

"And you are here to see someone?"

Her demeanor was probably what was required of this kind of a job, Armando thought.

"I'm here to see Sambra Gunnerson. She was brought in from a car accident. We understand it's a horrible accident, and there may be fatalities, and I just wanted to know—"

His legs began to give out. Coop grabbed him and held on. Everything was too similar to the night Gina passed away. He was glad they hadn't driven his truck, because he had his SIG and his long gun in the box beneath the driver's seat. He wasn't sure that he'd be able to stand getting bad news. He knew it would be the end of him. "Please, please, I need to find out if she's okay."

The nurse checked over a list of recent admits and found her name. Armando saw that her fingernail pointed to O.R.

"She's in surgery right now."

"So she's…?"

"I would say that does mean that she's still alive. They don't operate on dead people, sir." He wanted to jump over the desk and strike this woman. Instead, he inhaled and exhaled slowly five times, Kyle hanging onto his shoulder on his left, and Cooper with his arm around his waist on his right.

"Can we sit him down please?" Cooper asked. "This place is a zoo. Is there a waiting room for O.R.?"

"Tell me about it," she muttered under her breath. "I wish people would use those rooms right now." Stepping around the counter, she pointed to the red arrows on the side of the hallway. "You follow that, turn right, and you'll see a chapel. Right next to it are the doors leading to the operating rooms. You aren't allowed inside those rooms, but you can wait in the waiting room outside the doors or in the chapel."

Armando's legs were failing him again. He felt like he was going to pass out. Somebody handed him a bottle of cold water, which tasted delicious. He finished it in two or three gulps and dropped the plastic behind him in the hallway as they proceeded. Someone ran up to him and gave him another bottle of water, which he took and also drained.

"You're doing great, Armani. Just keep that up. Keep breathing. Let's get some more water in you. We're almost there," said Kyle.

Inside the small chapel, they helped him sit in the last pew. He rested against the arm of the pew briefly and then leaned forward with his elbows on his knees. Putting his head down between them, he inhaled and exhaled deeply.

Of all the events that had occurred over these last few weeks, again, he was unprepared for danger and harm to come to someone he cared so deeply about, someone who was an innocent. Again, he hadn't been there in time to save her. He should have never left her alone that night. He should have stayed and watched over her. Those thoughts ran around in his brain until he felt his body began to shake.

"He's going into shock, Kyle," Armando heard Cooper say.

"Go get something please. Get somebody to look at him," said Kyle.

Cooper left the room, and Armando's shaking continued. Kyle handed him another bottle of water, this time at room temperature. "You're doing just fine, Armani. Just drink. We're going to get you something for your stomach in a minute. But you just hang on, keep your head down, drink some water, and continue breathing. It won't be long now."

Cooper brought in one of the E.R. doctors who took a look at Armando and barked some orders to a male nurse standing nearby. They brought in a gurney, had Armando climb onto it even though he began to fight them, strapped him to the gurney, and covered him up.

"Fuckin' stop that!" Armando shouted, trying to fight with the nurse who was trying to cinch him up.

"Hold on there, buster," the doctor said. "Just trying to make sure you don't fall off and hurt yourself."

"Fuckin' get off me!"

Kyle leaned over him. "Stop it, Armani. They're here to help you. Be patient while we get you stabilized."

The doctor shouted. "I'm Dr. Davis, and I'm going to keep you comfortable. I'm going to make you warm, and I'm going to give you a little shot of something to settle your nerves, okay?"

Armando screamed, "No, I want to stay awake. I wanted to know about Gina!"

The doctor stood up and looked at Coop and Kyle. "Who's Gina?"

"His former wife. Long story. He's fine, doc."

Armando realized his mistake and corrected himself. "Sambra. It's Sambra. I need to see if she's okay."

The doctor patted him on the shoulder and said,

"We are working on it. We have a great orthopedic staff here. She's got a busted leg. It's right above her right knee, pretty bad fracture, and she's lost some blood, but she's pretty tough. And it could have been a lot worse, but I think she's going to survive."

Armando closed his eyes which were filling with tears.

"So now I've got you here, you're my primary focus right now, and I want you to get stabilized. You should start feeling better shortly."

"Goddammit," he muttered. "You sneaky son of a bitch. I didn't feel anything."

"Well, that's because Fred over here gave you the shot. You're too stressed out to even know what happened to you. That's why I'm going to keep you here for a few hours until you settle down. Right now, you're my primary concern. And as soon we get you out of the woods here, I'll go back to her."

"No, no, no."

"She's going to be okay, sir. You need to concentrate on lowering your heart rate, getting some fluids in you, and taking a little nap. That would be the best thing for you right now. Unless you're hurt somehow. Have fallen down or had some kind of an accident or an event?"

"No, I'm fine. Can I see her?"

"Well, she's not conscious. She's under anesthesia.

When she wakes up, we'll see. But right now, sir, you've got to put some effort into getting yourself feeling better. Can I give you some jello or some soup or something to settle your stomach?"

Armando was confused. He could feel the effects of something they must have given him. He was seeing foods dance through his eyes, jello, soup and ice cream, with music attached to it. And then all of a sudden, his eyes rolled back in his head and he fell asleep.

CHAPTER 30

S AMBRA WOKE UP to the bright lights overhead glaring into her eyes. It made the headache from before come roaring back to life, as well as the lump on the back of her head. She closed her eyes and squeezed them together, which didn't help. She tried to sit up but realized she was immobilized. A second of panic swept through her body, thinking that she'd been captured and strapped in some kind of a cell to a bed, held captive for ransom.

Her mind went crazy with all of the events of the last few hours.

She opened her eyes again, studied what was around her, and discovered it wasn't the back of a van or a dirty jail cell somewhere. It was a hospital room. And the immobilization holding her to the bed was from her right leg being elevated, braced under the knee and ankle with chains and a pulley attached the ceiling. She looked at her thigh, saw the heavy bandages, and noticed blood soaking into some of white linen and gauze. She tried to touch her leg with her hand, but it also was immobilized at the shoulder. She pulled and yanked until she got her arm out of the sling. When she touched her leg, it felt hot and was swollen to fifty percent greater than its normal size.

She pressed her head back into the pillow and sighed. Breathing the nice cool air from the hospital room with each intake and outflow, she was able to calm her nerves.

"I am alive. I survived."

The door opened, and Armando's face was the next thing she saw. His eyes were exhausted, red, and concerned. His hair, which was normally so perfectly combed in place, was slightly disheveled, but he still had that handsome smile, now with a shadow of a beard beginning to grow.

But none of that really mattered.

Her eyes began to water. "Oh my gosh, Armando. I'm alive. It's so good to see you."

He bent over her body and placed a kiss on her forehead. He had her head in both of his hands, rubbing her tears away with his thumb.

"Are you in pain?" he whispered as if she was a five-year-old.

"I'm fine. I'm just all trussed up here and can't move, but I'm not in pain. They probably have me injected with God knows what."

He listened intently to every word she said.

"Honest. I'm fine. You look terrible, but I'm still glad to see you!" she added.

His eyebrows tented. "Perhaps I should come back later?"

"Don't you dare! You sit right here until they throw you out!" she said.

Several minutes passed while Armando stroked her hair and tried to find a way to hold her hand. One of the positions he held caused a sharp pain, and she winced.

"Sorry. But this is supposed to be in a sling, sweetheart. Let's get that back in there," he said, adjusting the loose wrap to support her forearm, biting his lip and concentrating so acutely.

She loved watching every muscle of his arm, how delicately his fingers moved across her flesh. It felt so good to be in his company, to be touched by him.

"There," he said finally. "I worried so much about you. I am so sorry I wasn't there. I want to tell you, Sambra, that it was a mistake on my part to leave you alone, and I just wanted you to know that I want to take care of you. I want to help you get well. I want to—"

Sambra interrupted him. "Would you do that again please?"

Armando appeared confused. "Do what?" He scanned the bed, landing on her sling.

"Not my arm, silly. Would you kiss me again? But not on the forehead?"

Armando grinned, then sucked in air, gave her a silly half-smile, leaned over, and kissed her on the lips. She rose to meet him when he tried to pull away. So he deepened his kiss and then brought his hand up to her face again.

Her body tingled every place that wasn't numbed. The divine delight that spread, warming her heart, was so sweet and yet so powerful, she was at a loss for words.

"Sweetheart," he whispered.

It had now been twice since he'd said that word.

"Again, please," she begged.

He bent over and kissed her again.

"And say the word again. The S word."

He smiled. "Sweetheart. You like that word? It fits you."

"And I'm so glad that it does. You can tell me that as much as you like."

"Duly noted. I'm hoping you'll like other things I have planned for you as well. Just wait. I've been thinking about so many things."

She could see he was having difficulty with words. She smiled. "I've been thinking too."

"Go ahead. I want to hear."

"I'd like to learn more about you, Armando. I want to learn about where you come from, I want to meet your mother and father. I want to meet your little boy. I want you to tell me about your family, and I asked you if you would help me. Do you remember that?"

"Yes, I willingly accepted the challenge." He grinned, showing off those beautiful bright-white teeth.

"I want to learn how to be a good partner. I want to learn how to be a good daughter, a good companion, and a good wife. Will you help me with that too?"

"I will help you so much you're going to get sick of me. Honest to goodness, you're going to tell me to leave you alone. And even then, I won't. I promise." He rubbed her upper shoulder, massaging and kneading the muscle there. "What brought on this sudden desire to know so much about me?"

"Because I want to be part of your life, Armando. I know where I fit in now. I want to grow into the woman I could be, and that woman is beside you. I want us to heal each other."

OVER THE NEXT few weeks, they met and spoke often several times a day. She invited him to spend the night at her house, but he declined, asking for a little time, asking for her patience, which she gladly gave.

But on one evening, as they walked along the beath

together, something changed. It wasn't what was said, but she became aware that his arm and the side of his body were warmly and delicately enveloping hers, pulling her closer, as if he'd let down some gate and allowed himself to feel for her as a man. She knew his love for Gina was still there and always would be, but this particular evening was hers.

She asked him once if he was sure, as he removed her blouse and discovered she was not wearing any underclothes. His hands smoothed over her thigh and then over the leg that was healing, as he carefully positioned her, shed his clothes, and lay beside her.

"That's a loaded question, Sambra," he whispered in her right ear. "What do you think?"

"It's not what I think; it's what I feel. This is you, coming to me, asking if you can make love to me. And, Armando, I'm thrilled beyond belief. I want to be yours in every way possible."

His tenderness buried all her fears. In all her short years and many boyfriends, she'd never been so thoroughly worshiped as she was that night.

In the morning, when she awoke and found him sleeping next to her, she noticed that he'd removed his wedding ring.

CHAPTER 31

T RUE TO HIS promise, Armando told Sambra about his family, about his boyhood in Puerto Rico, and how close he was to his father. He introduced her to his mother and Gus Mayfield, the rock-solid former San Diego detective who had married her.

Artemis took to Sambra quickly, and the two of them told stories, drew pictures, and dug holes in the backyard together. He could tell Artemis was going to be as good for her as she was for him. And he didn't have trouble keeping his eyes from watering when he said to himself that Gina would want all this for him, for their little boy too.

He accepted that the fire and pain of the losses in his life made him a better person, not a person sucked dry by his pain. He offered to help counsel other SEALs on the teams, along with Dr. Brownlee, helping them or their families deal with the terrible hand Dr. Death sometimes gave them.

Sambra took him to visit her parents in Portland, where he stood up to her father who tried to convince him he was a good guy. He explained his worldview. Armando explained how what he did in the military helped him run his business in Portland, whether or not he ever appreciated it. And he told him that it wasn't important. He had all he wanted.

At the end of the visit, Armando could see that the man had changed, just slightly. He even acknowledged that he was an old hippie, "a work in process."

"Roger that, sir," he'd said.

Sambra's father liked that and wished them safe travels as they left.

They traveled to visit with Erik's parents, who were delighted to welcome Artemis and Armando into their family as one of their own. Sambra apologized for having made the distance between them and promised she wanted them to be part of their lives.

As they drove together, slept together, and worked on projects together, he began to see the wounded little child in her disappear, replaced by a confident, beautiful woman, stubborn and yet very kind. She also brought out the best parts of himself.

At last, it was time to bring her the present he'd been arranging for several weeks.

"I have a good friend coming over this afternoon. I'd like you to meet him. We served together."

"Of course. Who is he?"

"I'll let you see for yourself."

Tariq showed up right on the dot at two, as promised. He was a rather short man, with salt-and-pepper graying hair, no more than about five-foot-three inches. Armando'd forgotten how short he really was.

Sambra shook his hand and noted his Middle Eastern accent.

"Tariq was an interpreter we used in several of our missions in Syria and Iraq back over ten years ago now. We helped him immigrate to San Diego with his family, and he's brought many members of his family here over the years, right, Tariq?"

"Yes, I brought my wife's mother, who's ninety. We brought my sisters, one of their husbands, and two of their children. Sadly, we lost several. But I am most grateful to be able to share my new American citizenship with members of my family."

"That's wonderful. I was adopted as a baby from an orphanage in Syria. I'm not sure I'll ever meet any of my family, but I'm most grateful for being raised here. And I wish you and your family much luck and success. Do you plan to return some day?"

"We shall see," Tariq said and shrugged. "If I can be used as a force for good, I might be interested, but my military days are over. Today, I'm a farmer, and I run a vegetable stand at the local farmer's markets and flea markets all over the basin here. You must come and visit my little piece of paradise!"

"I'd love to," Sambra said.

"We would not have our family, our health, or the life that we live today if it were not for these fine gentlemen. And I pray for them every single day. Armando has said that you would like to learn about our culture, and I'd like to let you know you are welcome in my family anytime. My wife can teach you how to cook our traditional foods and tell you about our customs going back centuries. My children will probably drive you crazy, but my mother would love to have a new daughter to dote on. Won't you please consider yourself part of my Syrian-American family?"

"I would be honored, Tariq."

After the interpreter left, she ran up to Armando, tossing her arms around his neck. She was crying, and it was making him weep a bit.

"I never thought life could be so perfect."

"I meant it when I said I wanted to do everything in my power to take care of you, to help you heal. Because, sweetheart, that's what you've done for me. Believe me, this is only the beginning. Hopefully, it won't be so filled with danger, kidnapping, and bomb threats, but, if it is, well, we'll somehow weather it. I just know my place is here beside you, and that's never going to change."

"You have loved me for the woman I once was, the woman I am now, and the woman I'm turning into. There is no greater love than that, sweetheart."

Did you enjoy Grave Injustice? If so, won't you be so kind as to leave a review?

And, if you aren't familiar with the SEAL Brotherhood Legacy Series, the first two books in this series, Watery Grave and Honor The Fallen, are available by clicking on their links.

This new series follows the original SEAL Brotherhood Series, but takes a look at the couples and their families roughly ten years later, so it is an update on some of your favorite men and women.

And the original series, SEAL Brotherhood, is also available in two bundles, so you can read all 9 books and the two novellas that came first!

Ultimate SEAL Collection #1

Ultimate SEAL Collection #2

Almost all my SEAL books are on Audio under the Audible format, narrated by the talented actor and narrator, J.D. Hart. We hope you enjoy your exploration and let us know what you think!

ABOUT THE AUTHOR

 NYT and USA/Today Bestselling Author Sharon Hamilton's SEAL Brotherhood series have earned her author rankings of #1 in Romantic Suspense, Military Romance and Contemporary Romance. Her other *Brotherhood* stand-alone series are: Bad Boys of SEAL Team 3, Band of Bachelors, True Blue SEALs, Nashville SEALs, Bone Frog Brotherhood, Sunset SEALs, Bone Frog Bachelor Series and SEAL Brotherhood Legacy Series. She is a contributing author to the very popular Shadow SEALs multi-author series.

Her SEALs and former SEALs have invested in two wineries, a lavender farm and a brewery in Sonoma County, which have become part of the new stories. They also have expanded to include Veteran-benefit projects on the Florida Gulf Coast, as well as projects in Africa and the Maldives. One of the SEAL wives has even launched her own women's fiction series. But old characters, as well as children of these SEAL heroes keep returning to all the newer books.

Sharon also writes sexy paranormals in two series: Golden Vampires of Tuscany and The Guardians.

A lifelong organic vegetable and flower gardener, Sharon and her husband lived for fifty years in the Wine Country of Northern California, where many of her stories take place. Recently, they have moved to the beautiful Gulf Coast of Florida, with stories of ship-wrecks, the white sugar-sand beaches of Sunset, Treasure Island and Indian Rocks Beaches.

She loves hearing from fans through her website: authorsharonhamilton.com

Find out more about Sharon, her upcoming releases, appearances and news when you sign up for Sharon's newsletter.

Facebook:
facebook.com/SharonHamiltonAuthor

Twitter:
twitter.com/sharonlhamilton

Pinterest:
pinterest.com/AuthorSharonH

Amazon:
amazon.com/Sharon-Hamilton/e/B004FQQMAC

BookBub:
bookbub.com/authors/sharon-hamilton

Youtube:
youtube.com/channel/UCDInkxXFpXp_4Vnq08ZxM
BQ

Soundcloud:
soundcloud.com/sharon-hamilton-1

Sharon Hamilton's Rockin' Romance Readers:
facebook.com/groups/sealteamromance

Sharon Hamilton's Goodreads Group:
goodreads.com/group/show/199125-sharon-hamilton-
readers-group

Visit Sharon's Online Store:
sharon-hamilton-author.myshopify.com

Join Sharon's Review Teams:

eBook Reviews:
sharonhamiltonassistant@gmail.com

Audio Reviews:
sharonhamiltonassistant@gmail.com

Life is one fool thing after another.
Love is two fool things after each other.

REVIEWS

PRAISE FOR THE
GOLDEN VAMPIRES OF TUSCANY SERIES

"Well to say the least I was thoroughly surprise. I have read many Vampire books, from Ann Rice to Kym Grosso and few other Authors, so yes I do like Vampires, not the super scary ones from the old days, but the new ones are far more interesting far more human than one can remember. I found Honeymoon Bite a totally engrossing book, I was not able to put it down, page after page I found delight, love, understanding, well that is until the bad bad Vamp started being really bad. But seeing someone love another person so much that they would do anything to protect them, well that had me going, then well there was more and for a while I thought it was the end of a beautiful love story that spanned not only time but, spanned Italy and California. Won't divulge how it ended, but I did shed a few tears after screaming but Sharon Hamilton did not let me down, she took me on amazing trip that I loved, look forward to reading another Vampire book of hers."

"An excellent paranormal romance that was exciting, romantic, entertaining and very satisfying to read. It had me anticipating what would happen next many times over, so much so I could not put it down and even finished it up in a day. The vampires in this book were different from your average vampire, but I enjoy different variations and changes to the same old stuff. It made for a more unpredictable read and more adventurous to explore! Vampire lovers, any paranormal readers and even those who love the romance genre will enjoy Honeymoon Bite."

"This is the first non-Seal book of this author's I have read and I loved it. There is a cast-like hierarchy in this vampire community with humans at the very bottom and Golden vampires at the top. Lionel is a dark vampire who are servants of the Goldens. Phoebe is a Golden who has not decided if she will remain human or accept the turning to become a vampire. Either way she and Lionel can never be together since it is forbidden.

I enjoyed this story and I am looking forward to the next installment."

"A hauntingly romantic read. Old love lost and new love found. Family, heart, intrigue and vampires. Grabbed my attention and couldn't put down. Would definitely recommend."

PRAISE FOR THE
SEAL BROTHERHOOD SERIES

"Fans of Navy SEAL romance, I found a new author to feed your addiction. Finely written and loaded delicious with moments, Sharon Hamilton's storytelling satisfies like a thick bar of chocolate." —Marliss Melton, bestselling author of the *Team Twelve* Navy SEALs series

"Sharon Hamilton does an EXCELLENT job of fitting all the characters into a brotherhood of SEALS that may not be real but sure makes you feel that you have entered the circle and security of their world. The stories intertwine with each book before...and each book after and THAT is what makes Sharon Hamilton's SEAL Brotherhood Series so very interesting. You won't want to put down ANY of her books and they will keep you reading into the night when you should be sleeping. Start with this book...and you will not want to stop until you've read the whole series and then...you will be waiting for Sharon to write the next one." (5 Star Review)

"Kyle and Christy explode all over the pages in this first book, *[Accidental SEAL]*, in a whole new series of SEALs. If the twist and turns don't get your heart jumping, then maybe the suspense will. This is a must read for those that are looking for love and adventure with a little sloppy love thrown in for good measure." (5 Star Review)

PRAISE FOR THE
BAD BOYS OF SEAL TEAM 3 SERIES

"I love reading this series! Once you start these books, you can hardly put them down. The mix of romance and suspense keeps you turning the pages one right after another! Can't wait until the next book!" (5 Star Review)

"I love all of Sharon's Seal books, but *[SEAL's Code]* may just be her best to date. Danny and Luci's journey is filled with a wonderful insight into the Native American life. It is a love story that will fill you with warmth and contentment. You will enjoy Danny's journey to become a SEAL and his reasons for it. Good job Sharon!" (5 Star Review)

PRAISE FOR THE
BAND OF BACHELORS SERIES

"*[Lucas]* was the first book in the Band of Bachelors series and it was a phenomenal start. I loved how we got to see the other SEALs we all love and we got a look at Lucas and Marcy. They had an instant attraction, and their love was very intense. This book had it all, suspense, steamy romance, humor, everything you want in a riveting, outstanding read. I can't wait to read the next book in this series." (5 Star Review)

PRAISE FOR THE
TRUE BLUE SEALS SERIES

"Keep the tissues box nearby as you read *True Blue SEALs: Zak* by Sharon Hamilton. I imagine more than I wish to that the circumstances surrounding Zak and Amy are all too real for returning military personnel and their families. Ms. Hamilton has put us right in the middle of struggles and successes that these two high school sweethearts endure. I have read several of Sharon Hamilton's military romances but will say this is the most emotionally intense of the ones that I have read. This is a well-written, realistic story with authentic characters that will have you rooting for them and proud of those who serve to keep us safe. This is an author who writes amazing stories that you love and cry with the characters. Fans of Jessica Scott and Marliss Melton will want to add Sharon Hamilton to their list of realistic military romance writers." (5 Star Review)

"Dear *FATHER IN HEAVEN,*

If I may respectfully say so sometimes you are a strange God. Though you love all mankind,

It seems you have special predilections too.

You seem to love those men who can stand up alone who face impossible odds, Who challenge every bully and every tyrant ~

Those men who know the heat and loneliness of Calvary. Possibly you cherish men of this stamp because you recognize the mark of your only son in them.

Since this unique group of men known as the SEALs know Calvary and suffering, teach them now the mystery of the resurrection ~ that they are indestructible, that they will live forever because of their deep faith in you.

And when they do come to heaven, may I respectfully warn you, Dear Father, they also know how to celebrate. So please be ready for them when they insert under your pearly gates.

Bless them, their devoted Families and their Country on this glorious occasion.

We ask this through the merits of your Son, Christ Jesus the Lord, Amen."

By Reverend E.J. McMalhon S.J. LCDR, CHC, USN
Awards Ceremony SEAL Team One
1975 At NAB, Coronado

Made in the USA
Coppell, TX
16 August 2023

20423277R00194